Embracing
Amelia

by

Elaine Violette

Embracing Amelia

Cover Art by *The Wild Rose Press, Inc.*

The Wild Rose Press, Inc.
PO Box 708
Adams Basin, NY 14410-0708
Visit us at www.thewildrosepress.com

Publishing History
First Edition, 2023
Trade Paperback ISBN 978-1-5092-4892-6
Digital ISBN 978-1-5092-4893-3

Published in the United States of America

"What of Blakely's request for recompense?" Aunt Libby asked.

"The audacity of the buffoon." Eva huffed.

"Father told me about his insane request. He is aware of the viscount's self-indulgent nature. In his words, he would prefer to marry me off to someone else, but if I insist on begging off from every man who desires to court me, he shall have no choice but to choose my husband. At least he wants better for me than Blakely."

"Well then, what caused the half-hearted smiles and gloom today?" Eva asked. "At one point, you appeared on the precipice of tears before collecting yourself when duty called."

"I slept little after hearing the news. I was tired and, I suppose, embarrassed about the entire debacle."

Both her sister and her aunt did not know the truth about her injured ankle and Lucas's part in it. Her poor judgment of his character and her foolish imagining were hers to keep locked in her heart.

"We have a long night ahead. We should prepare for the dinner hour. I expect my mood will lighten with some needed rest."

Amelia chose not to add that news of Grey's forthcoming arrest might be even more satisfying than a good night's sleep.

Dedication

To my family, the treasured loves of my heart.

Chapter 1

"So unfair!" Amelia Pierce seethed as she brushed her horse's mane. "Once again I have wasted another Sunday afternoon watching men jump rails, conquer hurdles, and accept honors when I am just as capable to compete! No one will listen to my desires, Cinnamon, certainly not my family. According to society, I must marry, bear children, and be obedient to my husband, I am expected to be content to remain on the sidelines or stay at home and knit. My brother believes he is doing me a favor by allowing me to accompany him so I might glory in his win. I am sick to death of being only a spectator!"

Cinnamon rubbed her muzzle against Amelia's shoulder, drawing a disheartened but comforting sigh.

"Thank you for listening, my friend."

She gave a final sweep of Cinnamon's chestnut coat before hanging the finishing brush on the wrought iron wall hook. She expected Roderick would return to the stable soon, wearing his victorious grin and recounting his success.

"I think, sweet girl, this will be the last time this season we shall be his cheering section."

Cinnamon snorted at her words.

Despite her fury that had dissolved into gloom, she couldn't restrain a chuckle. "It appears you agree with me." Amelia tugged off a glove to wipe away tears.

"Why should you be stabled while eligible riders and their mounts prance about the rink wearing their pride like peacocks?"

Cinnamon eyed her before biting into a clump of hay.

"You are quite right. There is no use in complaining." As she drew her glove back on, her eyes widened. "My ring!" She pressed against the empty palm of the glove and each flattened finger. Then, stepping back, she gathered up her skirt and glared down at the thick bed of greenish-brown hay that covered the stable floor.

With a grimace, Amelia crouched and peered into the straw, hoping to see a gleam of emerald. The acrid smell of ammonia assaulted her nostrils. She moved back further, leaning on her haunches and then down on her knees. As she picked warily through the straw, she scrunched up her face at the smell and wondered if insects harbored in the hay. Her panic grew as she dug frantically into the damp fodder and tossed it away, tears running down her cheek.

A throat cleared above her. "May I ask what you are doing?"

Amelia's head shot up. Her breath caught and her heart jumped in her chest. She stared wide-eyed at Lucas Grey. Of all people who could have found her on her knees, why him? Grey's hands rested on his hips as he stood at the opening of the stall and gazed down at her.

She swept strands of hair from her face and tossed away a snared piece of straw that scratched her cheek. Taking a deep, uneasy breath, she straightened her bonnet that had slipped forward on her brow and sat up with as much dignity as she could muster.

"I believe it must be obvious," she snapped, brushing hay from her skirt. "I lost something. Why else would I be rummaging about in this filthy muck?"

"I beg to disagree, Miss Pierce. Fresh hay was added only this morning. However, even a well-maintained stable floor is not meant for a delicate nose. Perhaps you might tell me what you are looking for?"

His sarcastic tone and his mocking grin were more than she could bear. She huffed before plucking at another piece of straw that had attached itself to the lace on her sleeve.

"I lost my ring. It must have slipped off when I removed my glove."

"This ring must carry great value for a lady of your ilk to crawl around at the foot of your horse." He glanced at Cinnamon who remained still and watchful.

"Of sentimental value and an heirloom, well worth my humility."

"I commend your devotion. Allow me to assist." Lucas stepped into the stall and crouched down. "You are certain you lost it here?"

Amelia gaped at the darkly attractive and infamous stable manager who had given her barely a glance in the past. He was on his knees beside her ready to help. Thoughts of his scandalous reputation flew through her mind before her breath caught. His gaze, a deeper blue than her own, bore into hers as he brushed aside a wavy black lock of hair from his forehead. Realizing she had become spellbound, she shook her head and stared at the ground.

"Yes," she mumbled, recalling his question. "I am quite sure. I wear it always." She scoured another spot, hiding her flushed cheeks.

"I suggest you put on both gloves. Fleas and other insects tend to colonize in the straw."

She gasped and hunted for the glove she had tossed aside, found it half-covered with hay, and drew it on.

"What the devil is going on here?" A deep, familiar voice raged above them.

Amelia jolted, falling back into Lucas Grey's arms. She twisted, trying to scramble to her feet but her skirt caught beneath his leg. She fell into Lucas's firm grasp. Her chin jutted into his neck and her arms flayed before her hands found purchase on his forearms. She gaped at her brother.

Fury and disgust emanated from his scowl. He reached down, grabbed her, and pulled her to her feet. "My God, Amelia, look at you!" He turned his rage onto Lucas, who sat back against the wall of the stall, brushing straw from his shirt.

"How dare you touch my sister," Roderick spat, lifting his free hand into a fist. "You will pay dearly for this."

"Roderick, no!" Amelia screamed. "You misunderstand. He was helping me. I—"

"Silence!" he growled. He eyed the open stable doors. "The competitions are over. This place will be overrun with riders any minute. I need to get you out of here before anyone sees your appearance." His gaze darted to Grey. "I'll be back. You will answer for this." He dragged Amelia from the stable to his horse, lifted, and deposited her on its back.

"Cinnamon! We can't leave her!"

The sound of voices grew louder as a crowd headed toward them.

"I'll send a groom later."

Roderick mounted and rode swiftly away before anyone came upon them. When they were out of sight of Winston Stables, he slowed to a steady gallop.

"Tell me what happened," he demanded. "Did that bastard assault you?"

"No! I lost our mother's ring. He found me crawling on the stable floor and offered to help me search." She held her bonnet as she raised her voice over his horse's hooves pounding the rough path to their country house. "There is no fault, Roderick. When I pulled off my glove, my ring must have slipped from my finger. Please do not make this incident larger than it is."

"You were in his arms for God's sake."

"Not until you shouted and caused me to stumble."

Roderick heaved a loud groan. "Pray no one else saw you alone in that stall with Grey or your reputation will be in ruins. Your hat and hair were askew, and who knows what is caught in the fabric of your gown besides hay and grunge."

Amelia could think of nothing else to say. The wind grew colder and whipped at her face and hair. She was grateful Roderick said no more as they rode the final few miles to the Pierce country estate. Hopefully, he believed her and would let the matter rest.

Fortunately, the stable yard was empty when they arrived home. Her brother dismounted and helped her down.

"Go, get yourself cleaned up and presentable while I take care of my horse. Father shall decide how to handle the *incident* as you call it."

She grasped her brother's sleeve. "Must you tell

Father?"

"And how will you explain the lost ring? No doubt, he'll send a groom to search for it. I plan to have a drink to celebrate my win and…" He paused, tightened his lips and muttered, "Erase the vision of my sister in the arms of the Duke of Radford's bastard son."

Chapter 2

"Quilting is tedious. Utterly tedious. I refuse to stitch another stitch." Amelia jammed her needle into the cotton fabric and flung the section of quilt that had been draped across her lap.

"Ouch! You made me prick my finger." Eva, her older, married sister, sucked on her sore forefinger. "Quilting is not the cause of your annoyance. Father and Aunt Libby—shut up in his study for over an hour now—are the cause. You have been biting into your bottom lip for a good part of that time."

"Indeed, an hour, deciding my future. Amelia stood and straightened her skirt. "I am going in there."

"No, you are not." Eva grasped her sister's arm and tugged her back into her seat.

"They must allow me to explain. Father is in a rage for no reason."

"No reason? Roderick found you skittering about in the hay with that—"

"Do not say it." Memories of her brother's rough grasp on her arm as he tugged her off the stable floor reminded her of her humiliation. "And I was not '*skittering*' What does that even mean?" She glared at her sister before they both turned toward the open door of the small sitting room.

Their butler, Bidwell, stood at its entrance, clearing his throat. "My lady, your father awaits you in his study."

Amelia's lips twisted into a grimace at the grave look on Bidwell's face, a look so long, his usually round cheeks were stretched down to his chin. This was not a good sign. After giving Eva a panicked look, she followed Bidwell out the door and down the curved staircase toward the rear of the house. As she walked, she considered numerous arguments and pleadings to make her father understand. Although it did not appear so, the entire episode was innocent. Arguments rattling around in her brain silenced when they reached the study of Charles Pierce, the Earl of Weatherly.

Bidwell opened the door almost reverently and stepped aside. Amelia nodded, allowing the servant to go about his duties. Squaring her shoulders and lifting her chin, she entered her father's realm. He sat at his large mahogany desk, framed by oak-paneled walls lined with bookcases filled with rows of dull-colored tomes. A dreary day visible outside the long narrow windows appeared to mirror the grim expression her father wore.

She glanced at her white-haired, widowed Aunt Libby who sat rigid in one of the high-backed burgundy velvet armchairs angled in front of her father's desk. Pursed lips did not invite empathy.

She eyed her father, who sat forward in his well-worn leather chair, one finger tapping on his desk as if he had been waiting impatiently for her arrival.

"Sit," he ordered.

A chill ran up her spine despite the heat emanating from the blazing fireplace that gave an eerie brightness to the room. Her father's deep commanding voice and his creased forehead did not fare well for a good outcome. She obeyed, taking a seat opposite her aunt, while holding on to threads of hope she could escape her father's wrath.

"Amelia May, prepare to leave tomorrow for London with my sister. She has agreed to put up with you for as long as necessary."

Amelia shot forward in her seat. He could not be serious. "Father, we have only just arrived from London. I've just begun to plan the lavish menus and all the varied activities for our guests. I mean no disrespect, but I have much to do."

She held back saying that it was the first time she was in charge of holiday planning since her mother's death three years earlier. Her family was well known for the grand parties her mother and father had hosted during the weeks leading up to Christmas. This year her father felt ready to continue the tradition. He could not send her away now.

"I have made up my mind. You have ruined it for yourself. I can only hope that Roderick was the only one who saw you in that compromising position."

"I was not in a compromising position. I mean..." She bit into her bottom lip that felt raw from her nervous habit.

"Dear God, Amelia, you were in a horse stall of all places, in the very public and largest horse stable at Winston's arena, cavorting in the hay with that disreputable young man."

"I was *not* cavorting. Why does no one listen to me?" She heaved a frustrating sigh and looked toward Aunt Libby, who lowered her head at Amelia's beseeching gaze. She turned back to her father. "I was searching for Mother's ring. See? It is gone." She splayed the fingers of her right hand in the air. "The ring slipped from my finger when I pulled off my glove."

"And that is your explanation for scrounging about on your hands and knees with the Duke of Radford's illegitimate offspring? It is beyond the pale to even imagine the sight, its sordid implications, and possible scandalous outcomes. We must pray that Roderick was the only one to witness the sight. And what if he wasn't the first? I should never have allowed you to accompany him on his equestrian pursuits. The competitions leave him too busy to keep an eye on you. Of that, I take the blame." Weatherly pressed his lips together, gripped the arms of his chair, and sat back. "Is there more I should know?"

Aware of her father's heart condition and the longstanding animosity between him and the Duke of Radford, she tried to soften her tone. "Father, Mr. Grey and I have not spoken previously. He runs the stables and arena for John Winston. He goes about his business with seldom a word to spectators. When he saw me foraging in the hay for the ring, he offered to help. That was all there was to it."

"*Hmph*," Libby interjected and Amelia turned towards her. "Appearances matter, my dear." Her aunt returned to her prim-postured silence.

Amelia's shoulders sagged. No one would plead her case.

"The ring is lost then." Her father stared at Amelia's fingers, now clenched at her waist.

"We could hardly keep searching. Roderick lifted me off the ground and marched me out without allowing a word of explanation. I was not even allowed to return for my horse. He ordered a groom to fetch her. I was mortified."

"*You* were mortified? Perhaps you have not imagined what you might experience if anyone else saw you or hears of it. A ruined reputation, esteemed suitors turning away from you in disgust, or perhaps, a forced marriage to Radford's bastard. Did you consider any of the ramifications?"

Amelia bowed her head. "No, Father. I thought only of Mother's ring. I apologize. Please, do not send me back to London."

"I plan to send a couple of my groomsmen in search of the ring immediately. I do believe you were thoughtless, rather than prudent. Regardless, you behaved inappropriately, despite the reason." He pushed back his chair and stood to his full six feet. "Enough talk. You leave in the morning. My sister has holiday shopping to do. You will escort her while she keeps an ear out for any gossip about this incident. Pray there is none. She has promised to keep you too busy to get into any more trouble."

"Father, I beg you…" She pressed her palms to the edge of the desk, blinking away tears. "The holiday planning has only just begun."

"My decision is final. The staff can continue the preparations for our guests. Have your maid pack your immediate needs. More can be sent on later if necessary."

Amelia opened her mouth to object, but her father gave a dismissive wave of his hand.

"Elizabeth, I appreciate your assistance with my ill-disciplined daughter."

Aunt Libby gave her brother a respectful nod

before looking Amelia up and down. She paused at the rumpled laced hem of the simple white cambric gown. "I shall take her to my *modiste*. She appears in sore need of updated dresses. I imagine a new holiday frock would suit as well."

"If my daughter would spend more time in lady-like pursuits like Eva, instead of racing her horse through fields, or dawdling in a horse stall, I might be able to keep her in fashionable gowns. Use my accounts. Spend what you will. I expect her to look so dazzling at the Christmas gala that she will capture some fool's heart and be taken off my hands."

Chapter 3

Lucas Grey glared at his stepbrother, Graham Montrose, as they sat at a corner table in the Guardsman Pub, one of London's newest taverns. Graham suggested the place in Belgravia. He regaled Lucas on its infamous reputation of being haunted by a foot soldier savagely murdered after cheating at cards.

Graham, a schemer since childhood, never failed to have a store of information on the goings-on in London, including the most current scandals, or his pride-filled escapades, rubbing elbows with the elite. Telling him about Lady Amelia Pierce and the ring incident was a mistake.

Graham wore an expression of near sinister delight and expectation. "So, after her brother carried her off, you found it." He threw his head back and laughed.

"Keep your voice down," Lucas muttered.

He gazed about, grateful patrons were involved in their conversations. No one appeared to be observing them.

"You must admit there is humor in it." Graham lifted his tankard of ale, took a large gulp, and wiped his mouth, never losing his delighted grin. "You did not go after them?"

"They rode off the property before I found the ring. My mother was beside herself with worry when I told her what happened. She expected the Earl of Weatherly to be rapping at our door, demanding blood before the night was over."

"Never mind Lady Pierce's father's rage. I can only imagine the honorable Duke of Radford's wrath if he learns his bastard son caused the ruin of Weatherly's daughter."

Lucas grimaced at the mention of the man. He refused to call him Father. "I would probably be sent to the colonies never to return."

Graham snickered. "Despite his refusal to acknowledge you publicly, you must credit he has, at least, contributed to your upbringing. Few nobles bother to give financial support to illegitimate offspring for their formal education. I can understand why my stepmother might be upset at hearing her beloved son was found on his knees in the hay with a prominent earl's daughter."

"Mother is not responsible for my actions. Bad enough she has accepted the duke's money."

"Come now, Lucas, she had little choice. When my father was alive, he couldn't support you."

"Nor did he want to."

"True. As it was, my father gambled away my future inheritance, although it would not have been more than a pittance. I have had to make my way. At least yours cared enough for you to have a quality education."

"Cared?" Lucas sneered. "Pride, more likely, or some sense of ancestral honor. I concede that when he discovered he had impregnated her, he purchased our cottage and set up a fund to support it, with an allowance for my education. Mother never wanted to accept anything from him. I realize she had no choice at the time. Her family turned her out in disgrace. Mother took no satisfaction in his charity. She accepted it for my sake."

"How is Georgetta?" Graham asked with sincerity.

"She is faring well. She tries to do too much."

"I hope to visit one of these days. She was always good to me. I suppose she seldom leaves the cottage."

"A couple of times when she ventured out for a long walk, she lost her way. The doctor believes she suffered some mild brain damage from the carriage accident that may have affected her memory. Even after five years, she still has a noticeable limp and her eyesight in one eye is poor. Our housekeeper accompanies her if she desires to go beyond the garden, especially if she wants to take Molly out for a walk. The hound is twelve now. Her sight is worse than Mother's."

"Georgetta is a strong woman. She still treats me well, despite my father's cruelty. It was a blessing he died in the accident."

Lucas couldn't disagree. He had been fourteen and Graham twenty when his mother married Edgar Montrose, Graham's widowed father. He still remembered how Montrose appeared devoted to his mother before their marriage. Soon after the wedding, his true colors surfaced. He simply wanted comfortable living arrangements, and Lucas's father had provided that. He was thankful the man's death saved his mother from more abuse.

"She would never scorn you for your father's behavior, although you have tested her limits with your own." Lucas gave Graham a smirk that was more lighthearted than cruel.

"I credit her with patience. Your mother suffered under my father's tyranny, but I benefitted from her steady hand as well as from the refined education your sire provided for you. I learned to imitate your polish." Graham lifted his mug in acknowledgment.

"I credit Radford with nothing except, perhaps, a crumb of conscience for his desertion. Mother will not say a bitter word against him."

"My father believed she would do nothing to displease your father, and not just because he supported your fine education and welfare."

"What are you suggesting?" Lucas's raised voice drew the attention of customers from a nearby table. He tilted his head away from the curious stares, resting a fist on his cheek. "Explain your meaning," he said, his voice hushed, but not without anger at the implication of Graham's words.

"Calm down. If you want the truth, my father believed she never got over Radford. It was one of his excuses for finding other women to bed."

"Edgar Montrose never needed an excuse, and you know it. Enough talk about fathers." The conversation had turned in a direction Lucas refused to waste breath on. "I can support my mother now without Radford's charity. Recently, Winston alluded to a partnership. If Lady Amelia Pierce's father causes me to lose my position, then what?"

"Well, well," Graham chided. "Good fortune once again falls your way."

Lucas swore. He had unconsciously stirred up old jealousies.

He had looked up to his older stepbrother once, even followed him around, emulating his cavalier behavior and eager to shrug off his mother's overprotective nature. Graham took him under his wing early and taught him things his mother would have been shocked to learn. In time, he introduced him to ladies eager to share their bodies and expertise with a young lad. Eventually, he learned how Graham involved himself in disreputable schemes for extra cash or simply for adventure.

Lucas never knew if the money Graham used when they were out and about came from work, his drunken father's pockets, or a new scheme. Regardless, he had a soft spot for his wayward stepbrother. Despite his shadowy pursuits, Graham had a decent side. When Lucas's stepfather went into a drunken rage and mouthed off about his bastard birth, slapping Lucas with the back of his hand, Graham would push him aside and egg his father on to hit him instead. Lucas hated those times but felt indebted to him. In his youth, he enjoyed Graham's reckless side. If it were not for his mother's firm hand, he could have easily chosen to get involved in Graham's shady schemes.

"I doubt you need to worry about your job, Luc. You know more about good horseflesh and bargaining than Winston does. He would be smart to give you a percentage of the business." Graham emptied his mug and slid it over to the table's edge for the barmaid to fill. "I have some news for you. My future is looking brighter as well."

Lucas raised an eyebrow. "A legitimate future or another scheme?"

"You are prejudging me. I am engaged to be married."

Lucas's chin dropped. "I thought you swore off

shackles. Who is this naive woman?"

"Miss Annabel Whitcomb. Her father is in the clergy, the third son of the retired Right Honorable Lord of Parliament, Baron Whitcomb. Annabel is the apple of his eye, but she is growing long in the tooth. He is anxious to marry her off sooner than later. While he remains at the parsonage, he insists we live on his inherited property rather than my London accommodations."

"What accommodations? You are a recipient of generous acquaintances."

"I admit I might indulge in coloring the truth. I am past thirty and tired of my unsettled way of life. Annabel was engaged to marry once. Her betrothed begged off and married someone else, leaving her quite despondent and uncaring about her appearance, according to her father. In her melancholia, she added a few pounds, but I find her plumpness enticing. She is amiable as well as quite amorous. Her father is getting on in age and has feared she will remain a spinster."

"And you have wheedled your way into his good graces."

"He appears satisfied with her choice, and she is fervent in her devotion to me. We plan to marry before Christmas."

"That soon?"

"My future father-in-law has already posted banns, and the lady is anxious. I think she fears another rejection. I shall send you the date." Graham took another swig of his beer. "Now let me see that ring you found."

Lucas looked around the tavern. The last thing he wanted was to openly exhibit an expensive piece of jewelry. Further, seeing the hungry look on his stepbrother's face, he regretted revealing the find. His hurried visit to London had been unexpected. Winston had taken sick and sent him to keep his appointments that had been pre-arranged weeks earlier, leaving no time for him to return the ring. When his mother asked him to check on Graham while in London, he decided to meet with him before he became overly involved with his appointments. Perhaps it was the beer or even a mild pleasure at seeing Graham again that he told him about the ring. An error in judgment.

Grateful that the patrons at the nearby table had left, he pulled the ring from a concealed pocket in his coat. Graham reached for it, but Lucas drew it back, holding it snugly between his thumb and forefinger.

Graham's eyes lit up. "It is a beauty. An heirloom, I suspect. It will bring a pretty penny."

"I plan to return it to the lady."

"You are not serious. Weatherly could buy his daughter a dozen of them. You found it. Let me connect you to a discreet buyer. Just offer me a small percentage, a finder's fee."

Lucas knew well the conspiratorial smirk Graham wore. While Lucas inherited his father's darker complexion, coal-black hair, and according to his mother, the same brooding expression, Graham was blond, blue-eyed, gregarious, and a smooth schemer. Despite his drinking and careless living, his exceptional good looks and affable nature allowed him to move in circles above his station. He had acquired influential friends. Many took no issue with his suspicious transactions. He had no doubt Graham could find him a lucrative deal.

Elaine Violette

"You are over-thinking," Graham said, staring at the deep color of the emerald, encrusted with diamonds in a gold band. "I can find you a buyer before morning."

Lucas shoved the ring back into the concealed pocket of his coat. "You are pathetic. It is not mine to sell."

"Are you so well set that you would toss aside a good deal? You are far from sainthood. You take no issue in bedding wives of the aristocracy when their husbands are otherwise detained. Admit, it has been a game with you. You are not above making a profit on a ring, not stolen, but found."

"I do not seek out their attention. I take what they offer."

"I think it is your deep-seated way to mock your father's power and position. His bastard son tasting the forbidden fruit of polite society. With that jewel you have hidden away, you could add financial gain from their often-undeserved bounty. Besides, you could have returned it already. Yet, you brought it to London. You must have at least thought about selling it for profit."

"I was in a hurry to leave, and after the scalding glare I received from lofty-minded Roderick Pierce, I decided to wait a couple of days and let the incident cool."

"So, you did think about keeping it. Why not? If they are going to turn their noses down to you, you may as well take advantage."

A barmaid stopped to refill his mug. Graham winked at her, drawing a flirty smile.

During their interaction, Lucas dwelled on his stepbrother's words. It was true. He owed nothing to the nobility. He had overcome the shame that crept in when he first learned the meaning of the term 'bastard'. Still, he remained bitter at the way his mother had been disgraced while she accepted her lot and did her best to give her son a good life.

After the barmaid left to help other customers, Graham turned back to him. "You avoided my question. Why did you bring it with you?"

"I never planned to keep it."

"What else was I to think but that you were not considering selling it yourself?"

Lucas sat back and breathed out a heavy sigh. "The day after the incident, two of Lord Weatherly's groomsmen came to the stables. They questioned me as if I were a thief before spending the entire afternoon sifting through the hay. They had no idea where to begin their search. I offered no suggestions. I rather enjoyed watching them scavenge through the hay. It seems the earl offered a generous reward if they found it. They were not giving up easily."

Graham laughed before taking a swig of his freshly filled mug. "You are even more devious than I am. How long will you be in London, and where are you staying?"

"I only arrived this morning and must leave no later than Saturday. I plan to take a room at a hotel."

"Nonsense, you must stay with me. I have a friend away in the country who offered me a fine townhouse in Belgrave Square until he returns or until I am well situated with my new wife. I even have a butler and maid at my disposal."

"I do not know how you do it, but you always land on your feet."

"I think we have both learned, in different ways, how to overcome our disadvantages. I insist you stay with me. We have not seen each other in months. Let me give you a bed for a few days. You will be impressed by my quarters, and we can enjoy a night out together."

Lucas preferred to get his business done without revelry, but Graham was right. They had grown further apart over the past few years. He could at least accept his hospitality.

"Thank you. Give me the address. I have a couple of possibilities for some new business I want to check out this afternoon. Tomorrow morning, I have appointments to keep. I plan to get to bed early tonight. It was a long ride in. Thursday, I plan to go to the horse auction and if I can get everything done, I might be able to leave as early as Friday."

"Stay a few more days. Let me show you around. I can introduce you to Annabel. Or perhaps not. Your dark, brooding looks capture too many women's attention."

"I assure you I have no interest in capturing your lady's eye. We have an important event on Sunday that will bring in a tidy amount for the stables. With Winston laid up, I am in charge. I must get back."

"Then go out on the town with me at least one night. I know just the place. The women are delectable." Graham smacked his lips.

"Our tastes differ, and you easily forget that you will soon be a married man."

"Because you prefer the bored wives of polite society whose husbands are too old and limp to keep them happy?"

"They ask only for a good romp and discretion. Who am I to refuse?"

"I cannot argue with that logic. The handsome, illegitimate son of a duke under the silk sheets their ancient husbands pay for must make them heat up nicely."

Lucas stood and tossed a few coins on the table. "I shall see you later. Can you join me at the auction on Thursday?"

Graham winced. "I have been ousted from that event. I had a small enterprise that profited quite well for sellers, but, alas, the buyers became suspicious."

Lucas raised a hand. "Save me the details. See you tonight."

He left the tavern already regretting his acceptance of Graham's offer to stay with him. His stepbrother had a way of bringing Lucas's demons to the surface. He should have left the ring at home.

He pressed a hand to his chest and felt the ring's shape nestled in the hidden pocket. Was he indulging in a sick fantasy over having something that belonged to Lady Amelia Pierce in his possession? She was quite beautiful in a natural way, unlike women who feared smiling too broadly might cause a wrinkle or cringed if a hair fell out of place. Still, he did not take advantage of innocents, unlike Radford who had shamed his mother.

Lady Pierce was beyond his reach, but he had noticed her each time she and her brother came to the stables. He would like nothing better than to comb his fingers through those blonde curls tied back under her bonnet and hanging halfway down her back. Rummaging in the hay with her tantalized and tempted him, but he knew his place. He'd do nothing to harm his standing with his employer.

Grimacing, Lucas mounted his horse and rode off. When he returned home, he'd find a way to return the ring. Her brother was sure to participate in Sunday's events. She often came to observe. Would she be there?

He recalled overhearing her once complain to her brother about the unfairness of the equestrian competitions. She wanted to be jumping the obstacles along the course. Lucas had no doubt she could do it if she shed those long skirts. Her brother was most likely unaware she visited the facility some days at dawn, without a chaperone, and practiced jumping hurdles. She was an expert rider, even sidesaddle. He admired her daring and pluck to ride out alone at dawn. Beyond boarding prized horses, Winston Stables was strictly for equestrian training, obstacle courses, and competitions, a more acceptable venue for young ladies than racecourses like Epsom Downs in Surrey. Young ladies were expected to be properly escorted. Her choices, appropriate or not, were none of his business.

Why was he even dwelling on her? His mind should be on profitable business interactions. Not on Lady Amelia Pierce.

He picked up the pace and turned his thoughts to upcoming meetings.

Chapter 4

Since arriving in London the previous morning, Aunt Libby hadn't broached the subject of the stable incident. Despite her disappointment at leaving the country, Amelia was enjoying Aunt Libby's company. She found her aunt more relaxed and talkative when she was not in the company of her brother, the earl.

They had spent the past three hours shopping on Oxford Street. At Aunt Libby's insistence, she was fitted for three ball gowns, three daytime dresses, a pelisse-robe, and numerous accessories. Exhausted, Amelia was thrilled when her aunt suggested a stop at Gunter's Tea Shop.

"Amelia, speak plainly. What was truly going on at Winston Stables with that young man?"

Amelia's jaw dropped at her aunt's bluntness. "There is nothing more to tell." She groaned at having to repeat the same details over again. "I was brushing my horse down in the stable while I waited for Roderick. I admit I was not in the best of moods. I must have pulled off my glove with too much force, and my ring went with it. Lucas Grey, the stable manager, found me groping through the hay on my hands and knees. I did not expect him to get on his knees and help me search."

"And that is what he did."

"Yes. I was stunned and even quite rude when he

questioned what I was doing."

"Had he demonstrated disrespect towards you in the past?"

"We never exchanged words before. My brother warned me to keep my distance."

"No doubt Roderick's reasoning was to protect you from someone deemed unworthy of association."

"Grey always appeared industrious and focused on his work. I have overheard members of polite society be quite condescending to him, even addressing him as 'stable boy'. He ignores them and goes about his business." She stifled a grin.

"You find that humorous?"

"No, indeed. I think they are ill-mannered, flaunting their titles and positions. Although Grey has a sullen look about him, he appears to be a very diligent employee of John Winston, often at his side directing the activities."

With too much time on her hands as a spectator, her glances often drifted his way. In truth, there was something dark and mysterious about him, even dangerous.

Aunt Libby gave her a quizzical look as she sipped her tea. "I see from your expression that you have more to say."

She was too perceptive.

"I admit I have noticed women seek out Grey in a…flirtatious fashion, or with demure glances, even older married ladies of the Ton who accompany their husbands. Grey is undeniably attractive. He must seem a challenge to them."

"You have observed him quite closely, Amelia."

"Only because I have much time to observe since I

am not allowed to participate in the events."

She huffed just thinking of how she was delegated to the sidelines to watch men practice and compete. Her father and brother would be horrified if they knew of her visits to the arena at dawn to ride and practice hurdle jumping.

Aunt Libby leaned forward, her light blue eyes narrowed, emphasizing the fine lines and wrinkles that age had etched on her pale skin. "I see mischief in your expressions. What are you not telling me?"

Amelia fingered the handle of her teacup, wondering how much she could trust her aunt with her desires and secrets. She sat back and lifted her chin. "I am a competent horsewoman, Aunt. Father put me on a horse when I was barely able to walk. He has allowed me to go on hunts with him because he knows I am a skilled rider. He even commented once that I was a natural equestrian. He believes he is being generous by allowing me to watch my brother practice and compete at the arena. I want the privilege of participating, not spectating."

"Hmm." Libby took another sip of her tea. "You mentioned that you were in a mood when you lost the ring. Were you distracted?"

"I had spent more than two hours observing the trials, the competition, and male riders less capable than I am. I refused to watch any longer. I left to sulk with my horse who is forced to be stabled while others are being paraded around the rink."

Libby appeared sad and wistful as she set her cup down. "I understand, perhaps more than you think. My brother, as demanding and intimidating as he can be, has given you much more freedom than our father

27

would have ever allowed. Like you, my father expected me to display impeccable decorum and manners and be above reproach in all situations. I could never speak out of turn. Indeed, he would have preferred that I not speak at all unless I was addressed. For your father to allow you to go on a hunt and to credit you for your riding ability tells me he is at least amendable."

Amelia stared wide-eyed and with a new appreciation for her aunt's openness and honesty. Indeed, Aunt Libby must have been raised with the same high expectations and from what she was hearing, perhaps more stifling than her own.

"My attempts at rebellion brought severe punishment," Libby continued. "I spent much time in my room under lock and key and without dinner when I rebelled. My brother felt sorry for me. He sometimes sat behind my closed door talking to me and making me laugh without our father's knowledge." She smiled at the memory.

"I think my father would love to keep me in my room under lock and key if it were not for his desire for me to marry and get out of his gray hair," Amelia said.

"As a man who took advantage in his youth, he knows men's minds. Unfortunately, your mother passed before you became the young woman I see before me, leaving your father to prepare you for a future marriage. I believe he fears he may not be up to the task of keeping his fearless daughter safe and chaste. I do not believe your sister possessed such adventurous longings. You must admit most young ladies of your age and station are primping and posing in the hopes of capturing a husband, not dreaming of competitive riding." Aunt Libby lowered her eyes and gave a sudden sigh.

"What is it?"

"Rather than defending my brother, I should be asking for your forgiveness."

Amelia leaned forward, tilting her head at her aunt's admission. "I can think of nothing of which you need forgiveness."

Libby folded her hands on the ledge of the table, her shoulders sagging and the edges of her lips drawn down."Your father wanted me to move to the estate after your mother died so I could guide you, as your father put it. I refused. My husband and I had our lives and our friends. Your uncle was devoted to me and never attempted to stop me from whatever I desired to do. We had only one more happy year together before he died. When my brother took over the earldom and all the responsibilities that went with it, his demeanor was too much like our father. I had hoped that your mother's influence over the years had been enough to mellow his strictness. I knew you were well taken care of, and your married sister lived nearby."

"You are not at fault in any way. I suppose I sound like a spoiled brat. Father is not so terrible. I admit I push limits. My sister tells me I need to put a 'clip on my lip' a good part of the time."

"I think you may have inherited some of my feistiness," Libby said with a grin before growing serious again. "Amelia, you said that you know of Lucas Grey's background. Have you heard his story?"

"He is the Duke of Radford's illegitimate son. It is no secret. He has the blood of an aristocrat without the honor."

"Indeed, that is a good way of putting it. William

Sinclair, the present Duke of Radford, is Lucas's sire. He and I are close in age and often enjoyed the same round of social gatherings when we were young. I knew Georgetta Grey, Lucas's mother, but not well. She was not of our social standing. Her father was in the trades and was often hired to do work about our estate. When she and William fell in love—and I do believe they were in love—she was barely out of the schoolroom. When their relationship was discovered, William's father would not have it. He sent him off to university. Soon after, it was rumored that Georgetta was in the family way. She refused to admit who the father was, but there was much gossip about her and the duke's son."

"What happened to her?"

"Her family sent her away to stay with a distant relative in the country. We heard nothing more about her. A few years later, she returned to London with the child for her father's funeral. My husband and I attended the service. The boy's parentage could not be denied. Young Lucas looked so much like his father, even as a small child. He had the same dark features, aristocratic nose, high cheekbones, and cleft chin." Libby smiled at the picture that must have appeared in her mind. "By that time, the old Duke of Radford died, and his son, Lucas's father, inherited the dukedom. Of course, as a duke, he was expected to marry and sire a son sooner than later."

"And Lucas's mother was not a candidate."

"Never. The new duke's mother was a formidable woman. She had someone from an appropriate family picked out for him. From what I observed, he seemed to care little for making any attempts himself. His duchess was expected to be of the highest character and a member of the elite class. It is not uncommon for aristocratic men to have had indiscretions and to father bastard children. Common, but hushed. Not to be discussed in polite company. The duke's youthful transgressions were easily forgiven."

"Only the woman is shamed and cast off." Amelia shook her head, knowing her aunt spoke the truth.

"After Georgetta Grey returned to London," Libby continued, "gossip swirled that the duke visited her, even though he was betrothed, but they were only stories. His marriage took place, and Lady Miranda Platt became the new duchess. To his mother's dismay, Miranda had a difficult time becoming pregnant. When she finally birthed a child, it was a difficult delivery and a girl. When she became pregnant again, she lost the child. Her mother-in-law, who had been devoted to her, was waiting for her son to have an heir. She turned against Miranda."

"How terrible."

"Yes, but you must also know Miranda was a very difficult woman, quite vain. Not unlike her mother-in-law. She gave little attention to her daughter, Stephanie, and spent less time with her husband, preferring to be at their country estate when he was in London, and at their residence in London when he was at his country estate. There was little doubt it was an arranged marriage without love. She died a few years ago. The duke seldom participates in any events now, and when he does, he looks as if he'd rather be anywhere else. His daughter had her coming out, was betrothed, and has made a good marriage. I attended their wedding. It was the last time I saw the Duke of Radford in London."

"He and my father were in university together and were friends, once," Amelia said, "but they have not spoken in years. I have no idea why."

"It is not my place to tell you. I will say that both men are obstinate and set in their ways. I believe it comes from their strict training for the peerage and the responsibilities that come with it. Apart from their duties, many are dependent on them for their welfare. This is especially true for a duke who must please the king in all ways. Daughters may receive lesser attention and fewer privileges, but they also do not have to bear greater responsibilities. Your father will be much relieved when you marry. Speaking of marriage, you had a lovely coming out last spring, but I have not heard you speak of a special suitor."

"Father was disappointed I was not enamored by those who came calling. I am not ready for marriage."

"You hope for more freedom. I did too, but I found it after marriage. One day you shall meet the right one and married life will become more appealing."

Amelia's thoughts returned to Lucas Grey and a specific memory that rose more often than she'd admit. When she was on her knees, sifting through the hay, she looked up and met his gaze. He, too, was on his knees searching, but for that moment, they both stilled. It was why she remembered the color of his eyes so well. He spoke first and broke the spell. And it was a spell, a mesmerizing one. Discomforted by a fluttering in her chest, she had turned away from him. Roderick entered at that moment and roared at them. When she jolted and fell back into Lucas, she could not forget his hard, muscled arms securing her. Never had she been so close to a man or experienced such intensity of feeling.

It must have been quite a sight for her brother. Worse, when she tried to rise, her skirt caught beneath Lucas's boots. When she squirmed and twisted to free herself, he loosened his grip and she ended up nearly on top of him until her brother grabbed her arms and lifted her, none too gently. She still carried bruises on her forearms. The last sight of Lucas was seeing him sitting on the stable floor, watching her being dragged out the doors, his expression concerned, not mocking. How could she ever face him again?

"Elizabeth Forester, where have you been?" A tall, older woman, wearing a tawny brown, fur-collared coat, matching hat, and a mink muff hanging from her wrist, smiled brightly despite her scolding tone. "We missed you at Clara Loring's house on Sunday, Libby. As expected, she must be the first to hold her annual holiday tea."

"Yes, and putting us all to shame with her extravagance," Aunt Libby said, returning a welcoming smile. "Hello, Martha. So nice to see you. I was visiting my brother in the country. May I introduce his daughter, Lady Amelia Pierce? She is visiting me for a few days. Amelia, I do not believe you have met my dear friend, Mrs. Simms."

"Please call me Martha. Your aunt and I were schoolgirls together back in the day. Now we meet at teas, poetry readings, and sewing circles. There was a time when we stitched a bit of mischief together."

"Enough of that, Martha," Libby scolded.

"I would like to hear more," Amelia teased, drawn immediately to the woman's cheery, musical voice.

"Libby, you must bring your niece along Friday evening. You do remember our dinner party, I hope. No doubt an eligible bachelor or two will be present for your perusal, Lady Amelia." She giggled with almost childlike glee. "I do love to match make. You are not already spoken for, are you?"

"No, I—"

"Amelia, Martha has a way of causing many of us to blush at her utterances. Her husband Carlton is a successful London businessman and philanthropist. He is on the board of the local orphanage and has done wonderful work improving conditions there. Martha and I often visit and spend time with the children. We were busy knitting caps and scarves for them when your father ord… asked me to visit."

Amelia suspected she meant to say, he 'ordered' her to the estate to haul his wayward daughter to London.

"Of course, your dinner party. With my traveling, I admit it slipped my mind. I offered to bring my niece to London for some holiday shopping." Libby pointed to their purchases. "We shall be there and, Amelia, the gown being delivered tomorrow will be perfect for you to wear."

"How fortunate that I stopped in here," Martha said, giving her aunt a pointed look. "I might not have forgiven you, Libby, if you had been absent at my table without a word, Or, perhaps," she placed her forefinger to her chin, "I would. Our memories are not as good as they used to be. I am trying to remember why I walked in here in the first place." Martha laughed. "It is a pleasure to meet you, Amelia, and I look forward to seeing you both Friday evening." With a bright smile, she went on her way.

"I hope you don't mind I accepted the invitation for

both of us."

"Not at all. I…liked your friend immediately."

"There was a pause in your words, Amelia."

"I am enjoying our time together, but I do hope I can return to the country soon."

"Soon enough, my dear." Libby reached across the table and patted her hand, offering a sympathetic smile.

On the ride back to her aunt's townhouse, Amelia stared out the coach window, frowning. She loved her aunt, but she missed the country and morning rides on Cinnamon. She had been so excited about her plans for the holiday season, now left to the staff.

Instead, she would be primping for a dull dinner party with her aunt's lovely but elderly friends.

Chapter 5

Staying with Graham had become a chore. He stayed up until the wee hours of the morning and slept until the afternoon. He was disappointed, even irritated, when Lucas refused to join him in his nightly carousing or drink with him until dawn. Graham relished living out his remaining bachelor days with gusto. Lucas had business matters on his mind.

He appreciated the comforts available in the luxury townhouse Graham had somehow managed to use as a temporary residence while a wealthy lord was off to the country. Admittedly though, a small, dingy hotel room might have given him more peace of mind. Listening to Graham's boasts of his exploits was draining. He was glad to leave the house today before Graham stirred.

His meetings so far went better than expected. He'd managed to secure two young mares and a Morgan that would be the pride of the stables. Thursday in London was the horse auction at Tattersall's. He looked forward to checking out the available stock. With only a couple of appointments left the next morning, he hoped to be on the road by Friday afternoon.

He arrived at the sales yard of Tattersall's at Hyde Park Corner at noon. Finding a worthy addition to Winston's inventory was hit or miss at the auction, but he found it invigorating talking to other men who trained horses or were well educated in horseflesh.

When he entered and observed the clientele, he recognized Mr. Holmestead, a banker he had met with the day before. Holmestead was talking to another man in the center of the wide circle of horses being paraded around. When he saw Lucas approaching, he waved him over.

"Grey, just the man who can help. Have you met Carlton Simms?"

Lucas looked at the older man, tall, slim, with a neatly trimmed white mustache and beard and dressed conservatively in a dark green long coat and top hat. He stood eye-level with Lucas's six-foot-one stature. "I haven't had the privilege." He offered his hand. "Lucas Grey."

"Pleased to meet you, young man," Simms said with a welcoming nod. "Although your name is new to me, your face is familiar. Do you have a brother, perhaps?"

"No, I have no natural siblings." Lucas saw the question in the man's eyes and wondered if he knew the Duke of Radford. His resemblance to his father annoyed him.

"Lucas manages the Winston Stables and knows about fine horseflesh, Carlton. He is the one to ask about that hunter you are considering. He trains horses and runs many of the competitions at the arena there. If you have never visited Winston Stables near New Market, I recommend it."

"Winston's, yes." Simms rubbed his short beard. "I have heard of it but have not been there. I shall remember your recommendation, Holmestead."

"You have your eye on a particular horse?" Lucas

asked, grateful that his banker associate had steered the conversation away from the other man's curiosity about his appearance.

Holmestead had been doing business with Winston for years and knew of Lucas's parentage.

"Yes, I enjoy fox hunting immensely with friends in Kent, but I am a guest using their horses and hounds. I have never owned a hunter. My wife thinks I have lost my marbles coming here today, but I am quite determined. Not right to depend on good friends to supply a seasoned horse to carry these old bones. Martha will just have to deal with it. I want one I can trust not to toss me over at the sight of a rabbit or squirrel."

Lucas figured Simms was past sixty, though his eyes held a lively glimmer. He appeared in good physical health but at his age, he needed to take great care in picking the right horse.

"I was talking to a gentleman on the other side of the yard. Ah, there he is." Simms pointed to a short, stout, black-bearded man bringing a bay around.

Lucas frowned. He knew the trader and his reputation. On the surface, he gave the impression of being honest, genuine, and affable, but he had no problem falsifying a horse's abilities. He could easily take in an uneducated buyer.

"What do you think, Grey?" Simms asked. "The man says he is a good hunter, calm, and trustworthy. Exactly what I am looking for. He told me I am just the man he would trust with him. He loves the horse but must sacrifice him."

"Really? Money issues?" Lucas could well imagine the story this professional trader told Simms.

"His health will not allow him to ride anymore. Says he has a son who wants the horse and is angrier than riled-up hornets that he is being sold. Has no trust in the boy to take care of him. Called him a lazy, good-for-nothing. He made it clear he is not going home with the horse." Simms gave a plotting grin. "I think he is desperate enough to make a deal. How are you at judging a good price?"

Lucas knew enough about dishonest horse traders to know this was one of their ploys, using children or desperate circumstances to get rid of an animal. "I can haggle if it is a sound investment."

"I can attest to Grey's shrewdness." Holmestead chuckled. "He haggled a good deal from me."

"Well then, could I beg a few minutes of your time to take a look at the bay?" Simms asked.

"Will the trader allow you to take the horse on a trail before you commit? We can meet tomorrow early afternoon, take the bay out and give him a run." Lucas already knew the answer.

"He was regretful when I asked. He hoped not to take the horse home and face a run around with his son. He has another interested buyer coming back later this afternoon."

Lucas was not surprised, and he doubted the seller spoke of truth. "Let me examine the animal and then we can consider his price."

The three men strode across the yard as the chestnut bay was being secured to a post. When Simms approached, the man broke into a wide smile, until he saw Lucas.

"Peabody, haven't seen you around for some time," Lucas said, his hands splayed on his hips. "Mr. Simms here tells me you have been ailing, and you must part with this fine horse. What a shame."

Peabody's grinning lips twitched down before he recovered and nodded. Simms and Holmestead gazed at each other. Simms scratched his beard while Holmestead's brow furrowed.

Lucas sauntered over to the horse and circled him slowly, gauging his height, the length of his back, his hindquarters, and hooves. The horse was calm, too calm. Lifting his bridle, he looked thoughtfully into his eyes before moving to the horse's rear. He had seen enough. This was a young crossbreed, not too big, with a good shoulder, and sedated. This was no seasoned horse and most likely skittish. Why else would the man medicate the animal?

He returned to face the trader. "This horse has been drugged," he said, loud enough for everyone around to hear.

Onlookers paused and watched the scene.

"What? No, no, he has been out in the sun all mornin'. He's tired. That's all." The trader eyed Simms. "You ain't going to find a better horse here today for your needs. I'm ready to give you a fair price."

Simms glanced at Lucas who lowered his eyes and gave a grim nod. "I believe I will pass."

The trader swore as the three walked off.

"Sorry I could not offer better news," Lucas said when they reached the entrance to the sales yard. "I know of Peabody and traders like him. Unfortunately, too many unwitting buyers are taken in by their tactics. I will keep an eye out for a seasoned hunter for you." He reached out to shake Simms's hand. Simms took it and placed his other hand on Luke's shoulder.

"Young man, I thank you. Please excuse my ignorance. I'd have made a foolish purchase, trusting the man's demeanor rather than knowledge. You have saved me from my wife's scolding and possibly some broken bones." He smiled. "Will you be in London long?"

"No, I must get back as soon as possible. We have a large event on Sunday. I planned to leave at dawn on Saturday, but if my meetings wrap up early, I may be able to leave tomorrow afternoon."

"Might you consider keeping to your original plan? I want you to be my guest at a dinner party my wife and I are having tomorrow evening. Holmestead will be there as well as other notable London businessmen. Perhaps I can thank you by introducing you to prospective clients. Allow me to show my gratitude for your help."

"Thank you, but I—"

"Furthermore," Simms said, "my wife tells me her dearest friend is bringing her lovely niece, making our party thirteen." Simms waved a finger in the air. "Not a good number at all. You can help me once again by attending."

"Lucas, I suggest you not miss one of Simms's dinner parties. You are bound to make some profitable contacts," Holmestead urged.

"I understand this niece is delightfully attractive too," Simms added with a wink.

Lucas had no desire to even out odd numbers. A dinner party was low on his list of entertainments, next to being fashionably pleasant and accommodating for someone's most likely dimwitted niece. Spending a night with his stepbrother held less appeal.

He had run out of excuses to decline Graham's insistence on showing him his London haunts. More enticing was meeting possible business contacts for his employer. John Winston was more than a boss. In many ways, he was a father figure who Lucas respected and admired and who trusted him enough to consider a partnership.

"I shall look forward to it." He hoped he sounded somewhat enthusiastic.

"Excellent!" Simms reached into his pocket. "Take my card with my address. I shall see you at seven. At our age, my wife and I no longer party into the wee hours of the morning. I promise you will still be in good form for your trip back on Saturday morning."

"That would be ideal. Good day, gentleman." Lucas walked away relieved by Simms's last words.

He had already planned on an early exit.

Chapter 6

"Do not expect peerage to be present, my dear, but wealthy men of business along with their wives," Aunt Libby said as they traveled by carriage to the Simms's townhouse on Friday evening. "You will find the company less formal in their conversations, but don't mistake the casual atmosphere or their occupations as a statement of less wealth or influence on London society. You may meet retired lawyers and barristers, those who have made their wealth in shipbuilding or trade, others who come from ancient lineages, have great wealth, hold government posts, and are included in the landed gentry. They may not have titles, but their intelligence and industriousness have been rewarded. I suspect you shall find the company less stuffy than the teas that wives of the peerage have invited us to in the next weeks."

"Weeks?" Amelia's mood plummeted. "How much longer must I stay in the city? There is still so much to do in the country for holiday planning. I trust the staff will be well prepared for meals and housekeeping needs, but the activities for our guest's enjoyment are in my hands, at least they were."

"I understand your disappointment, my dear. The accepted invitations should reveal if any gossip has circulated about your unfortunate incident. Nothing has come to my ears yet, but time will tell. Now you must erase that glum look on your face and try to enjoy the evening." Libby looked out the window as the carriage slowed. "I see we have arrived."

As the footman helped her down from the carriage, Amelia noted the refined elegance of the terraced townhouses, not so unlike her father's London townhouse in Mayfair. Libby's friends were most definitely well off. The nobility of society would be insulted at her comparison.

A butler greeted them at the door and led them into the foyer. As he gathered their cloaks, Amelia glimpsed the dining room to the right of the ground floor entrance. The long dining table adorned with tall candles, linens, sparkling silver, and porcelain dishes revealed understated elegance. Flames from a finely carved, marble fireplace and the mauve-colored walls gave the room a soft, welcoming atmosphere.

The butler led them up the staircase with its delicately scrolled, wrought-iron balusters to the first floor. A chorus of voices and laughter rose as they ascended, very unlike the stuffy dinner parties of the older peerage she was too often forced to endure. This was at least a welcomed change. She wondered if they were the last to arrive. Had her aunt planned to be fashionably late?

Martha and Carlton Simms greeted them immediately with broad smiles. "Delighted to see you and looking so well, Libby," Carlton said, taking her aunt's hand in his own. "And this must be your beautiful niece who dazzled my Martha!"

Amelia smiled at the older man whose good-humored, flirtatious manner caused his wife to roll her eyes. The warm affection between the two was immediately obvious.

"Mr. and Mrs. Simms, it is a pleasure to meet both of you."

"Martha and Carlton will do, my dear," Martha chirped. "I am thankful you were both able to join us. Libby will introduce you to our friends. Almost everyone is here. I must be off to check on dinner preparations."

As soon as Martha Simms left them, a woman of a similar age to her aunt and with silver ringlets about her highly rouged cheeks approached them. Simms stepped aside, nodded pleasantly to the women, and walked off.

"Libby, I was disappointed to receive your note declining my invitation." Her disapproving tone did not match her set smile.

"Clara, I do apologize. Martha tells me your tea was lovely as always and your season's decor splendid." Aunt Libby offered a smile that did not appear to alter the woman's mild irritation. She seemed to want more of an explanation, but her aunt did not offer one.

"And who is this?" Clara asked, giving Amelia an assessing look.

"Allow me to introduce my niece, Lady Amelia Pierce. Amelia, Mrs. Clara Loring."

"The earl's daughter?" Clara's smile brightened. "How is your dear father? Has he returned to London for the holidays? Perhaps I can entice you both, and your aunt, of course, to come to a small gathering next week? Are you staying at your father's London address? I shall send an invitation tomorrow."

Amelia gave her aunt a wary glance before replying. The humorous expression her aunt wore, hidden from the woman's buttery words, said volumes.

"My father remains at our country house. I am enjoying a stay with my aunt, a brief visit only."

Aunt Libby reached for Amelia's arm and tugged her toward others in the room, rescuing her. "Please excuse us, Clara. I want to introduce my niece to Mr. and Mrs. Randall."

They moved on, leaving Mrs. Loring with her mouth open.

"She is a gossip, a busy body, and a social climber," her aunt whispered. "Say as little as needed with a smile."

Amelia stifled a laugh. Just what she was thinking.

After more introductions, Libby stopped to have a conversation with Mrs. Adele Hornsby, a ship builder's wife. Amelia found her especially warm with a congenial nature, easy smile, and quite beautiful for her mature age. She was impressively dressed in cerulean blue silk that brought out the pale blue of her eyes. Her black hair with threads of silver was swept up in a sophisticated coiffure and pinned with a jeweled clip. Amelia hoped she could be as striking as this woman when she reached her elder years.

"What a beautiful gown, Lady Pierce," Mrs. Hornsby commented with awe in her tone, reaching out, with a delicate hand to finger the sheer crème taffeta on Amelia's sleeve. "That shade of violet overlaid by this exquisite taffeta is breathtaking. Libby, the lace trim has the markings of Madame Lorraine. Am I right?"

Libby chuckled. "Indeed, Adele. I know we both enjoy her mastery over needle and thread. Amelia, Adele as you can see, has an eye for fashion much more than I. Perhaps, when you return to London for the

Season, Adele might join us on a shopping trip."

"We must add that to our calendars. What a delightful afternoon that would be."

As Mrs. Hornsby continued, a tall, distinguished gentleman with a trimmed gray beard and mustache, and receding hairline drew up behind her aunt. Amelia noticed a glimmer of a smile and eyes that appeared meant only for her aunt. Was she imagining it? He gave her a gentle tap on the shoulder.

"Albert. I was not told you would be a guest. Lovely to see you."

Libby's eyes sparkled and her usually pale skin took on a faint blush. Mrs. Hornsby gave a knowing smile and turned away to speak to another guest.

"When Carlton told me you had returned, I could not stay away," the gentleman said, grinning. "I assumed I would be your dinner partner, but I heard you returned from seeing your brother with this attractive young lady."

"My niece, Lady Amelia Pierce. Amelia, Dr. Albert Curtis, a physician much admired in London, and a dear friend."

"No flattery, please. I am happy to make your acquaintance, Lady Pierce. I believe we have met before." His words held a jovial note.

Amelia liked him immediately and sensed a kind, fatherly nature, ideal for a physician. "We have? I am sorry. I do not recall."

"You would not. At your birth, young lady." He laughed. "Your mother, God rest her soul, went into labor during her stay in London. I was called in. Was it eighteen or nineteen years ago?"

"I turned twenty this past April."

"Albert, you never mentioned this before," Aunt Libby remarked.

"At my age, and with so many patients through the years, I do not always recall every event, but your introduction stirred my memory. If I remember correctly, it was in the middle of the night." He grinned at Amelia, before turning to Libby. "I did not have the pleasure of knowing you then. You were well married at the time."

Yes, Dr. Curtis was quite smitten with her aunt. Either that, or he was an old flirt.

Chapter 7

"Why did I agree to this?" Lucas grumbled as he tied the ivory neckcloth borrowed from his stepbrother.

He'd forgotten to bring an extra one in his hurry to leave for London. His Friday appointments had run later than expected and he was forced to dress in record time for the Simms's dinner party.

Last night, Graham's butler had pressed the tailcoat, trousers, and shirt he had packed. Now he just wanted to get this night over with so he could get back to the stables and to the well-worn shirts and buckskin breeches that served his purpose most days.

Adjusting the standing collar of his waistcoat and combing his fingers through his hair, Lucas hustled down the stairs and out the door.

As he walked the few blocks to the Simms' residence, he reviewed all he had accomplished while in London. His boss would be pleased. Winston wanted to retire soon and had no sons to take over the business. He had made it clear, not on paper, but in words and appreciation, that he wanted Lucas to manage and, perhaps, have at least a percentage of the business. Winston respected him and cared nothing for his ignoble past.

At least tonight's dinner, according to Simms, was to entertain business associates and their wives. When events included members of the peerage, one or another too often recognized Lucas's name and history. If he began a conversation with one of their daughters, she was politely whisked away. If they only knew it was their wives who whispered to him or passed him notes to meet them in a private location.

As he neared his destination, he fidgeted with his cuff and inhaled a frustrated breath. He could have been traveling home tonight. He hoped this dinner party was not a waste of time. He'd been glad to steer Simms away from a deceptive deal and didn't expect gratitude or a social invitation. Sellers like Peabody tarnished the profession. Too many gullible buyers were taken in by men like him, and too many horses were used and sold for the wrong reasons. Lucas often met people he didn't like, but never a horse. Most of the time he preferred being in the company of horses rather than men who thought more of themselves than they deserved. He had encountered enough idiots with royal blood who he had less respect for than the animals he worked with daily.

Both Simms and Holmestead greeted him when he arrived. Mrs. Simms, he was told, was off checking on the dinner preparations. The two men introduced him to Arthur Struthers, a London lawyer, who inquired about Winston's Stables and the training facilities. While Simms went off to speak with other guests, the three men carried on a spirited conversation that promised future possibilities for business. It appeared the evening might prove lucrative and better than dealing with his stepbrother's urgings to spend a night on the town.

Struthers's wife, Cecile, soon joined them. After introductions were made, and with only a few words, the woman succeeded in changing an invigorating discussion into a social calamity.

"Arthur, I just had a lovely conversation with Libby Forester and her niece." Turning to Lucas, her warm smile and glint in her eyes held more than pleasantries. "You, young man, should stroll over and introduce yourself. It appears that Lady Amelia Pierce will be your dinner partner. Between you and me," she said conspiratorially, "the earl's daughter rebuffed more than one suitor after her coming out last year. News spreads, especially about such an intriguing, young woman. Of course, I said nothing of the gossip to Libby's niece."

"That would not have been appropriate, Cecile." Struthers raised his monocle that dangled from a chain and gazed about the room.

Lucas, stunned by her admission, hoped he'd succeeded in appearing unaffected. He followed Struthers's gaze, past the open doors of the next room that created a larger area for guests to gather. If she was present, she was out of their view.

"She is the Earl of Weatherly's daughter," Struthers remarked. "Our host has matched you up well."

Lucas said nothing, still grappling with the news. Amelia Pierce was the last person he expected to see in London. He pressed a hand to his chest before remembering he had changed into his more formal wear. The ring was in the pocket of his traveling coat, left behind at his stepbrother's lodgings.

"Please, excuse us," Mr. Struthers said apologetically, to Grey and Holmestead. "Cecile, re-introduce me to Mrs. Forrester. I want to ask after her brother. Perhaps, you would like to join us, Grey, and meet this young lady."

"Lucas, I'd like to hear more about this weekend's events," Holmestead said, "if you can spare a few minutes before being introduced to your dinner partner?"

"I apologize. What did you ask?" Lucas forced his attention back to their conversation. "Oh, yes, you wanted to know more about the riding schedule on Sunday. Are you thinking of attending?"

Before Holmestead could respond, their host appeared, calling all the guests to dinner. Everyone from both rooms moved toward the stairs. Lucas held back to complete the conversation with Holmestead and more so, to avoid the confrontation with Amelia Pierce. They were the last to descended to the dining room below.

Simms, who stood at the bottom of the staircase, waited for Lucas. "There you are, Grey. I want to introduce you to your dinner partner."

Amelia, who stood outside the dining room chatting with her aunt and the doctor, turned sharply at Simms's words.

"I am pleased to introduce you to my newest acquaintance," Simms said to the small group, as he rested a hand on Lucas's shoulder. "Meet Lucas Grey. Grey, I am happy to introduce you to our dear friend, Mrs. Elizabeth Forrester, and her lovely niece, Lady Amelia Pierce, the daughter of Charles Pierce, Earl of Weatherly. Ladies, this young man saved me yesterday from buying a steed that could have been my demise. He recognized the horse I nearly purchased had been drugged to appear quite docile." He grinned broadly at Amelia. "I believe my wife has placed the two of you together at dinner."

Simms, distracted, as other guests crowded into the dining room, missed Libby's wide-eyed glare and Amelia's gasp. Lucas did not. Either Mrs. Forrester was aware of the ring incident or knew his background. Perhaps both.

"Mrs. Forrester." Lucas made a brief bow before turning to Amelia. "It is a pleasure to see you again Lady Pierce."

"Ah, you have met!" Simms said with delight.

"Lady Pierce often accompanies her brother to Winston Stables." Lucas kept his gaze on Amelia.

The shock on her face at seeing him was replaced with a nervous smile.

Simms held out a hand toward the dining room. "My wife will scold me if I detain you any longer."

****

Only four seats remained on one side of the table as they entered. Dr. Curtis led and pulled out a chair next to his. Libby grasped Amelia's arm and directed her to sit next to the doctor while she took the seat Lucas had drawn next to his own. Amelia caught the odd glances from guests situated across from her. Clenching her hands beneath the table, she forced a pleasant smile before focusing on the table settings and flickering candles.

As servants offered bowls of white soup, the men at the table conversed jovially. Most of the women remained silent, allowing Amelia time to slow her racing heart. He was here. Not in her wildest dreams could she have imagined this moment. Here she sat, near Lucas Grey, at a London dinner party only days after falling into his arms on a stable floor—a moment she'd spent too much time dwelling on. She lifted a spoon to her lips, swallowed too quickly and choked on a sip of soup.

"Amelia?" Her aunt patted her on the back.

"I'm fine," she raised her napkin to her lips, cleared her throat, and lowered her eyes to avoid onlookers. How was she to get through this night? It was enough that Aunt Libby purposely sat in the chair meant for her. That act alone was enough to create whispers. What must her aunt be thinking? And what was Grey doing here?

As bowls were removed and platters of veal, chicken, and vegetable dishes followed, Amelia managed only a few bites of each dish set before her but tasted nothing. She cast an occasional glimpse toward Lucas when she dared without her aunt's notice. He appeared serious and mostly silent as those around him carried on conversations. She had never seen him dressed in evening clothes and he wore them well. Was he as uncomfortable as she, and what must be going through his mind? Perhaps nothing concerning her. He was all business from what she'd observed in the past. He may have simply seen the stable incident as humorous and thought nothing more about it. She drew a slow, calming breath, knowing she must stop dwelling on him as if they were the only two in the room and everyone else background noise. Aunt Libby gave her a sudden nudge, pulling her from her thoughts.

"Dr. Curtis has asked you a question," her aunt murmured discreetly.

Blushing with embarrassment, she turned his way. "I apologize, Dr. Curtis. I was…What did you ask?"

"No apologies, my dear. Elder conversations can be boring to the young."

"Oh, no, not at all. I was wool gathering for a moment. Please, what did you ask?"

"I was wondering how long you plan to stay in London. Perhaps I might have the pleasure of taking you and your aunt out for luncheon next week."

"A few more days. With the holidays coming, I must return to the country sooner than later."

"Then you have much on your mind." He gave her a fatherly grin.

Amelia nodded, grateful when another guest drew the doctor's attention. As a servant placed a light fruited custard before her, Amelia stole another glance at Grey. Mrs. Struthers, a prattler, sat on Lucas's other side and appeared to carry their conversation, Amelia nibbled at the dessert as the discourse flowed around her until the meal ended.

Much praise was extended to the host and hostess for the fine dinner. The men stood as the ladies prepared to leave for the drawing-room. Amelia paused for a final glimpse of Lucas as she followed her aunt from the room. Their eyes met, but he quickly turned away when her aunt reached for her arm. Shortly after taking a seat in the drawing-room, Aunt Libby complained of a headache. They gave their regrets and were out the door within minutes. Her aunt barely spoke on the way home and went immediately to her room when they arrived.

Relief flooded Amelia. She hurried upstairs, shut her bedroom door, and rested against it, grateful to be alone, and fearing what tomorrow would bring.

****

Lucas stayed for a polite amount of time before telling Simms he needed to have an early start home in the morning. Simms was enough of a gentleman not to comment on Elizabeth Forrester's odd behavior. Lucas suspected they would be the subject of conversations when he left.

As he walked back to the townhouse, he spent less than a minute on the coincidence of seeing Amelia and much longer on remembering the vision of her in a pastel silk gown with filmy material draped over it that did little to hide her slender form beneath. Her hair, usually pinned back beneath a bonnet at the stable grounds, was swept up with a gathering of golden curls cascading down. He wanted to pull out the pins that held the mass of curls and do much more. After Sunday's events, he must find a way to return the ring and wipe her from his mind.

Thankfully, Graham was still out when he arrived back at the townhouse. He breathed a sigh of relief. He was tired and disturbed at seeing Lady Pierce and the uncomfortable events that followed. After stripping off his evening wear, he packed up his belongings and laid out his traveling clothes. It was past midnight and he planned to leave before dawn for the long ride back. Unable to stop envisioning Amelia, he reached into the hidden pocket of his riding coat to finger her ring in his hand while he remembered the feel of her, falling into his arms on the stable floor.

Lucas stilled. The pocket was empty.

He shuffled through other pockets, despite knowing he had not placed it anywhere else. Could it have dropped on the floor? He searched around the bed, under it, and in every crevice. Gritting his teeth, he suspected what he did not want to believe. Would Graham stoop to this level? He swore before throwing on his shirt and trousers. He knew a couple of Graham's haunts. He had to find him.

It was four in the morning when Lucas returned. He sat hard on the parlor couch, pressed his elbows into his thighs and rested his head in his hands. He found no sign of his stepbrother. His work required him to be back at the stables by noon and it was over a three-hour ride.

He mulled over what he would do to Graham. But what if he didn't take it? There was no other explanation. He had kept it secure. There was no sign a housekeeper entered during the few hours he was at the dinner party. Slouching back against the sofa cushions, and despite his need to stay awake, sleep overtook him.

A door slammed, jarring him awake. Lucas shook off the remnants of troubled sleep. His stepbrother stumbled through the hall.

"Graham!"

He stepped back and shot a glance towards the parlor. "Lucas, I thought you'd be gone. I…I am not feeling well," he mumbled, grabbing the stair railing. "I need sleep."

"No, we need to talk, now." Fully awake and fury building within him, Lucas crossed the threshold into the hall.

Graham lifted his bloodshot eyes before lowering them. He began climbing up the stairs. "I drank too much. Not a good time to talk."

Lucas grabbed his arm, and pushed him back against the wall. "Where is the damn ring? What did you do with it?"

"Luc, please, I have been out all night. Let me rest awhile."

"I see the guilt on your face."

He seethed, teeth clenched. Fisting his hand, he thrust it beneath Graham's chin. His face distorted in fear. Graham stumbled, landing on a lower step. Sucking in his rage, Lucas stood over him.

Graham wiped saliva from his open mouth. "Luc, you know it was worth a great deal of money. I could not let you. I was going to see a dealer today. Find out the value."

Lucas opened his palm. "Give me the ring."

Graham squeezed his eyes shut, tilting his head as if he expected a blow. "I drink too much. You know that about me. I do foolish things. I'm sorry, truly sorry."

Lucas leaned down and grabbed his shoulders, shaking them until Graham had no choice but to look up into his eyes. "What are you saying?"

"I...lost it."

"What?"

"I didn't mean to."

"You lost the ring? Where?"

Rage dug deep into Lucas's chest. Rage, not only at Graham but at himself. He had known better than to tell him about the ring, to trust him in any way.

"In a poker game," Graham whimpered, lips quivering. "The man cheated. I know he did. I had the best hand. I was out of blunt. I should have won."

"You lost the ring in a card game?" Lucas snarled.

"He cheated. Believe me. I am sure of it."

Grabbing Graham's neckcloth he twisted it, tighter, as Graham's face turned red, his eyes bulging. Loosening his grip, he shoved him back against the stairs, swore, and slammed his own fist against the wall.

"Please understand. I should have won."

"Who has it, Graham?"

"I don't know the man's name. He's the son of an aristocrat and throws his weight around," Graham bellowed. "Obnoxious and arrogant. They call him the viscount." He combed his hands through his hair. "I don't know his name. Shows royal blood doesn't breed class." He pulled and loosened his neckcloth before dropping his head into his hands.

"I need a name."

"I don't know! I never played poker with him before. When he asked to join the game, I figured he had money to lose." He lifted his gaze. "When I accused him of cheating, he laughed in my face. Nobody would take my side. Not against his wealth and breeding."

"Damn you!"

"That's all I know. I could recognize him, but how would I get it back? You said yourself the girl thinks the ring is lost. She is no more the wiser, right? For God's sake, she's an earl's daughter, Lucas. Think of your mother. Your father, a noble, shamed her and you. Why would you want to return it? Keeping it would have been one more way to spit at those who treat us like we're nothing. It should have been sold yesterday. I am only sorry that I don't have the value of it to give you. You'd be going home with pounds in your pocket."

Lucas pressed his lips together to contain his fury. If he did not leave now, he might beat the living hell out of him. It would do no good. He needed to get back to the stables. He had been foolish to trust Graham. What else could he have expected from him?

Sidling around Graham's slumped figure, he climbed the stairs to gather his things. He had put stock in the better side of his stepbrother, and he'd proved his uselessness once again. Turning at the top of the steps, he gazed down at Graham who remained at the bottom, sniveling. Nothing more could be said.

The ring was truly lost.

Chapter 8

Saturday morning Amelia entered the breakfast room, wondering what to expect from Aunt Libby. No doubt her aunt's distress and fear of possible repercussions led to their abrupt departure. Her own astonishment left her in a daze and gave her a sleepless night.

She poured herself a cup of tea from the sideboard and took a seat, thumping her fingers against the table. She could only imagine what the other guests thought of her aunt's maneuver. That alone, apart from their sudden departure after dinner, must have caused all manner of gossip after they'd left.

Twenty minutes passed before her aunt entered the breakfast room, fully dressed. Not in her usual morning gown but wearing the same teal carriage dress she had worn when they left for London.

"Good morning," her aunt said with lips pursed, as she strolled to the sidebar and poured a cup of coffee.

"Good morning." She waited, saying no more until her aunt took her seat. She wondered only briefly if she had forgotten an event, a luncheon perhaps. "I see you are dressed for traveling. Have I missed something?"

"We are returning to the country. I sent my maid to pack your things."

"Today?"

"It is for the best."

Amelia was still taken aback. She was thrilled, of course, to return home. At the same time, guilt flooded her for causing her aunt so much trouble.

"Amelia, is it possible Mr. Grey followed you to London?"

"Of course not. How would even have known that I left the country? You must have noticed that he appeared as surprised as I was that we had both been invited. I heard it said that he is in London for business. No doubt, it was simply a coincidence."

"Regardless, if he is here, we shall not be. Your father would never forgive me if I unknowingly caused us to cross paths with him again. What if the young man spoke of the incident to others last night? Could you imagine? While the men were off drinking their port, he could very well have made a joke out of your ring search. These were men of business, some with chatty wives who have little concern for how gossip could ruin your opportunity for a good marriage. If the story is passed on to their wives, I shall most likely hear of it. I was up half the night worrying about who may have been a recipient of his, perhaps, distorted side of the story."

"I highly doubt the incident would be brought up in conversation. Mr. Grey is a serious-minded, silent sort, not one who demonstrates bravado. From what I have observed, he is not a petty conversationalist."

"My dear, you are being naive. Although he is not responsible for his scandalous birth, he has earned notoriety. Often, it is the quiet ones of whom we must be wary."

"I don't understand."

With a sigh, Aunt Libby pushed her cup away.

"You mentioned you have seen ladies—married ones—seek him out at Winston Stables. That news came as no surprise. Rumors abound that he has been—how can I say it—attentive to a few of the bored wives of the ton, some who flaunt their indiscretions. Rumors that he is a rake of the first kind are tasty morsels on the lips of the gossips. Some, I daresay, who may be jealous that he has not bedded them."

"Aunt Libby!"

"Forgive my bluntness, but I speak the truth. Heaven forbid that your name should be on the tip of their tongues."

Amelia rested her elbow on the table and her chin on her cinched fingers. She considered her aunt's words. She had witnessed the flirtations. Women, regardless of station, could be drawn to his dark looks and demeanor. She certainly was, though she would not admit that to her aunt. Not only was he attractive, but he exhibited a vitality difficult not to notice.

She envisioned him corralling horses or working in the stables with sweat on his brow, his black, wavy hair falling across his forehead. His manners were not polished like the men her father would approve of, like Herbert Mason, who had asked for her hand after her coming out. When she had rejected his proposal, her father refused to speak to her for days afterward.

"Seeing Lucas Grey last night brought to mind his mother." Aunt Libby fingered the rim of her cup. "I wonder how she is coping. I have not seen her in years."

Her words drew Amelia away from her wandering thoughts. "You mentioned that you did not know her well."

"I was acquainted with her, but we did not move in the same circles, of course. Georgetta visited London with her son a couple of times after her father's funeral. I had heard this though I did not see her. It was suspected that she was tired of hiding away. Gossips noted that she held her head high and showed pride in her son. She eventually married, you know, but not for the good from what I gathered. She is a widow now and not in the best of health. I heard she was seriously injured in a wagon accident. Her husband, who was at the reins, was killed. He was drunk, lost control, and they went down a hillside."

"How terrible. She has had a difficult life."

"Indeed, I hope she is doing well. Her son was fortunate to receive a quality education. At least the duke saw to that. Lucas Grey is the image of his father. I saw that again last night. I am sure others at the gathering who know the duke noticed as well. They would have been too polite to say anything. For Georgetta, her son must be a daily reminder of her transgression." Libby shook her head as if she were trying to toss the memories aside.

"He appears well respected at Winston Stables."

"Do you go often?"

"Father allows me to accompany Roderick and observe his practices and competitions." Amelia was not ready to tell her about her early morning rides to the arena's tracks, which were only a few miles from their estate.

At first, when she saw Grey walking about the place with the owner, John Winston, she feared they would question her presence or say something to her brother. They never did. They went about their business and let her ride around one of the rinks and practice jumping.

"I have already told you how I feel about the competitions being for men only."

Libby nodded as if she well understood Amelia's feelings. "You say he is respected at work. You have observed others' behavior toward him." Her aunt's eyes narrowed before she took a sip of coffee and a bite of her toast.

"He is often with the proprietor and runs many of the daily operations since Mr. Winston is getting up in age."

"Men of business respect hard work. It appears Georgetta did a fine job raising him. Too many advantaged sons of the nobility can be lazy and see little value in working with their hands. Your Uncle Everett, being a man of business, would become upset when he observed how the privileged were determined to keep those below their station in their place."

"As we women are kept in our place?" Amelia added, with more of a pout than a direct question.

"My dear, it is not at all the same."

"Indeed, it is. I can hear my father's voice in my mind. 'Amelia, you must have a chaperone when out alone, a groom to accompany you on all rides. You must be above reproach in all your conversations at public gatherings. Stop slouching! Keep your head erect.' Aunt Libby, it is exhausting. Even with marriage, Father must approve of the man I choose." Amelia crossed her arms tightly to her chest and pinched her lips. "I may never marry."

"You are headstrong, my dear, but I believe when the right one comes along, you will change your mind."

Libby pushed back her chair and stood. "Our conversation has been enlightening, but I can no longer avoid the reason for our departure today. Prepare to leave within the hour. I need to figure out how I am going to explain our sudden return to your father."

****

Amelia groaned as she sat at her writing desk and browsed the list of guests who would be arriving later in the week. She was forced to add Viscount Blakely to the list after her father informed her that he would take the place of Lord Ellington's wife. The Marquess and his son would be arriving on Saturday, but his wife was on an extended visit with an ailing sister. Amelia needed to make certain she was not paired off with Viscount Blakely at dinner or any other time. She had been a victim of his leering gaze and overabundant flattery in the past.

Today was the first time since returning to the country two weeks ago that she'd felt confident about her preparations for their upcoming guests. Apart from overnight visitors, three couples from the local gentry would be coming for the holiday ball the first week of December. One of the couples planned to bring their unmarried daughter, Genevieve, a school friend of hers.

Amelia put the pen to her lips, a possibility crossing her mind. No, she should not in good conscience wish Blakely's affections on her friend, especially since Genevieve has set her sights on her brother, Roderick.

Pushing thoughts of the irritating viscount aside, she continued perusing her list. Lord Hastings and his wife, Lady Lenora Hastings would also be arriving on Saturday. Amelia paused at her name. Although her husband, along with Lord Ellington, was one of her father's hunting and fishing friends, Lady Hastings was a busybody and a notorious gossip. Lady Catherine Hampton would be arriving on Sunday with her mother, Margaret. Lady Hampton's husband sent his regrets late last week since he was fighting a lingering cold. He wrote of how pleased he was that his wife could escape London for a time. Amelia was aware that he and his wife seldom spent time together, so sending his regrets did not come as a surprise.

The widows, Lady Sarah Hartmann and her sister, Dora, were also Sunday arrivals. Both women had been dear friends of Amelia's mother. Aunt Libby, her sister, Eva, and her husband, Drake, brought the guest list to eleven for guests staying for an extended time. Amelia, her father, and her brother made an even number fourteen, not counting neighbors coming only for the holiday ball.

Setting the guest list aside, she browsed the menus. Thankfully, Cook, who had been with the family since Amelia's childhood was fastidious in her preparations. Amelia trusted her choices while planning daily events and the holiday ball had filled Amelia's every hour. She had not minded the work, but she needed a break from the busyness.

Amelia set down her pen and gazed out the window at the gray, November sky. The garden below, its bushes clipped and neat, was no longer surrounded by flowers, instead fallen leaves blew about in the wind. A ride in the brisk air would be heavenly. She pushed the menus aside. Could she steal away without the company of a groom for a few hours? She contemplated her escape.

Servants were busy preparing the guests' bed chambers. The housekeeper, Mrs. Wesley, was overseeing the polishing of silver. Father was meeting with his stewards behind closed doors in his study. He would be busy for hours. Cook and most of the kitchen help had Monday afternoon off. Perhaps she could get away unnoticed.

"Is there anything I can do for you, milady?"

"Good afternoon, Jenny. I was doing a check of the menus. Everything looks fine." She rose, putting her hands to her lips to stifle a yawn, more for the maid's benefit. "I am going to my room. I may take a nap."

"You have been busy, miss. Take a good rest. Tomorrow will bring other troubles. Francis said we could be getting our first snow in the morning. The temperature is dropping. There's a chill in the air."

"Snow, so soon?"

"Our head gardener should know. He has been covering the plants he is worried about."

Enough. She slid her chair beneath the escritoire. "I shall spend the remainder of the afternoon in my room. Please tell Edith I do not want to be disturbed until dinner." The last thing she needed was to have her maid rushing to her room to turn down her bed or insist that she change.

She waited for Jenny to leave before climbing the staircase to her room. In minutes she changed into her riding habit, laced up her short boots, and donned her hat. The hall was empty of servants and the house quiet when she slipped out of her room. Taking the back stairs, she stepped quietly past the servant quarters and out the back door. She knew the best path to freedom since it wasn't the first time she had slipped out of the house in secret.

When she reached the stables, only Henry was sitting by the door, whittling. Ideal for her escape. Being the youngest of the stable hands and least experienced, he was usually given the responsibility of watching the stable early in the morning or when there was little activity. To her advantage, Monday afternoons usually meant time off as well for stable help and grooms.

"Henry, did you hear snow may be coming tomorrow?"

"Yes, miss. Everything's stowed that needs to be. November winds have been in a fury, but it's still too early for a snowstorm. I ain't expecting much."

"Wonderful. Cinnamon needs exercise. No need to call a groom. I am just using the paths around the property."

"I'll have her saddled and bridled and brought out quick for ya."

Amelia smiled. Henry, shy in her presence, never asked questions or narrowed his eyes like other stable help when she insisted on riding out alone.

Cinnamon whinnied when she saw her, obviously happy to be outside. Amelia was grateful for Henry's help today, although she was quite capable of mounting Cinnamon herself. She used the sides of her stall; her method when she escaped at dawn before the house was awake.

As Henry held Cinnamon steady before the mounting platform, she settled on the saddle, one knee through the pommels and the other in the stirrup. He handed her the reins and waved her off. She'd gotten into the habit of wearing riding breeches beneath her skirt, offering modesty, but also allowing her to ride full saddle when no one was about to chastise her.

"The heavens are with us," she whispered in Cinnamon's ear as they trotted away for Henry's benefit.

Once she was out of his sight, she led the horse into a lively canter. She laughed with joy for the first time in what seemed like ages, from the exhilaration of the ride and brisk air.

She should have found time sooner to ride, but she had wanted to prove to her father she was up to the task of planning the events for their guests. After her return from London, there was no more talk of the lost ring or Lucas Grey. Her father had other concerns and accepted her aunt's excuse that she had engagements that would leave Amelia little to do on her own in London. Aunt Libby reported to him that she had not heard any gossip about the incident. She did not find it necessary to tell him of their unexpected meeting with Grey. She had returned to London but would be back for the holiday events.

With little thought to consequences, she turned toward the shortcut she knew well and headed toward Winston Stables. Riding at a good pace, she could arrive in less than half an hour. The final arena event of the year had taken place the previous weekend. The training rings would most likely be empty, especially on a chilly day at the beginning of the week. At least that was her hope.

Mr. Winston was aware that she broke the rules of feminine decorum when she appeared at dawn without a groom and before he opened for business. He had even stopped to watch her on occasion. She had never dared visit in the afternoon before. With winter weather approaching, this might be her last chance to practice jumps until Spring. The thought of a final practice before winter approached filled her with delight. Nothing could remove stress more than the challenge of hurdles and jumps.

She had proven to her father during hunts that she could jump low obstacles without unhorsing herself. She could only imagine what he would say and do if he knew her early morning rides were not simply exercising Cinnamon on the paths around the estate. Riding sidesaddle had its limitations, but she was confident in her abilities. Admittedly, Lucas Grey and the incident came to mind, but she tossed it aside. She had, at most, an hour to practice before the sun began to set or before anyone would miss her.

This was her time.

Chapter 9

Lucas cursed as he tugged at the rusted wheel bolt on an old hay wagon that had been left idle for years. Mrs. Winston insisted that the wagon must be decorated for the holidays and placed at the entrance of the property.

The last thing on his mind was holiday decorations, especially since the arena was closed for the season. The final Sunday events had been successful and lucrative. While horse owners appeared occasionally to check on their boarded stock, now was time to concentrate on maintenance, winter storage, care of the stock, and ordering equipment, feed, and supplies. The kind of productive work that kept him from thinking of personal issues.

The heat of his anger toward his stepbrother remained. Graham was right about one thing. The Earl of Weatherly could well afford to buy dozens of expensive rings. He owed them nothing. Yet, the memory of Amelia Pierce's desperation to find the ring and the feel of her shapely body before her brother wrenched her from his arms remained vivid. He had to put her and the entire ring incident out of his mind. It was believed to be lost. Even if Graham could track down the man who bested him in the poker game, he would never get it back.

He had to put the entire fiasco behind him.

Lady Amelia Pierce, on the other hand, was more difficult to forget. The enticing vision of her at the London dinner dressed in that shimmery gown with the fetching neckline was unforgettable. Her flaunting of tradition when she rode to the stables to practice in the early morning hours, heightened his desire to know her better, in all ways.

Lately, dreams he had cast away years before pulled at him. Despite a well-deserved reputation of self-indulgence with women who had no issues with a secret dalliance, he no longer had a taste for the game. In the past, he gloated at the idea he could embarrass his father. But even that did not give the pleasure it once had. He was twenty-eight years old. His occupation and the privileges John Winston afforded him had awakened dreams of respectability he had cared little about in the past.

Too often loneliness crept in at night when he was too tired for busyness. Needs that he could not fill on his own brought helplessness he disdained.

"Damn," Lucas growled, more at his thoughts, than the stubborn bolt he hammered, trying to loosen the crud and rust that held it in place.

He needed to focus on his work.

"You still at it, Grey?" Tom, one of the maintenance workers approached. "Why not leave it for the mornin'? I need to head home. My wife's birthday is today. If I don't give her a couple of hour's relief from our three little tyrants, there ain't going to be any peace for me tonight."

Lucas pulled himself up from his haunches. "You go on. You did a fine job fixing that broken gate. That horse wanted out and nothing was going to stop him."

"His rider didn't know what he was doin'. All's well now." Tom pulled off his hat and combed back a mop of dark hair peppered with gray that fell forward on his brow. "There's a lady ridin' about the west training ring. She's a good rider but an odd sight. Her riding costume speaks privilege, but no groom in sight. The sun's gonna be settin' before long and the weather's turnin'. Do you want me to tell her to leave? Don't want to brush velvet the wrong way if you know what I mean."

Lucas groaned. It was probably Eliza Swinton.

"I will handle it. Go on home." Lucas waved him off.

Swearing, he brushed hay from his trousers. Mrs. Eliza Swinton, who lived a mile from the stables, was unhappily married to a man twenty years her senior, an arranged marriage to a friend of her father's. Lucas had made the mistake of spending one drunken night with her when her husband was in London. Most of the women he chose to bed saw him as a secret diversion. In public, they were the epitome of loyalty and respectability. They knew who buttered their muffins, despite wanting a forbidden scone on occasion. Eliza Swinton had become too obvious of late.

A few weeks ago, she had arrived alone late in the afternoon asking him to help her with a riding technique. As the daughter of a member of the gentry who was an ace equestrian, she had been schooled in proper etiquette and horsemanship. Her demeanor made it clear it was not a horse she wanted to ride. He began to suspect that she wanted to get caught in a flagrant affair so her husband would divorce her. Lucas did not need that kind of publicity or an enraged husband at his throat.

After grabbing his coat, he led his stallion from his stall, then mounted bareback, and rode toward the west training ring, the farthest one from the main arena. The wind had picked up and the sky looked threatening. Snow might be coming sooner than later, and he might be forced to escort her home.

Was that her plan?

Chapter 10

Amelia rode about the ring a few times before attempting a jump. She felt well balanced in the saddle and had complete confidence in her horse.

The side leather was a shorter length than most side saddles, making it safer when jumping. Her only concern was that a couple of the jumps were higher than she had attempted in the past. She frowned. Better to ride astride, but it was too late now.

Cinnamon had the strength and coordination to take jumps, but how would she do with higher rails? Amelia circled the ring again, taking two of the smaller jumps. How she loved being here, away from the confining structures she must follow at home. Her horse had become her closest companion. Time seemed to stand still when she was out for a run. Now a niggling thought about the time disturbed her pleasure. Gazing up at the sky, she sensed she had been away too long.

"What do you think, Cinnamon? Shall we attempt it? I know you can do it."

A couple more jumps and she had to head back if she was going to make it before dusk or before her absence was noticed.

Cinnamon, in fine spirits, jumped over the smaller rail. Amelia picked up the pace and jumped easily over the next higher one.

"Good girl!" Amelia laughed.

The final one was even higher. The wind was picking up and her exhilaration rose with it. This afternoon's ride cleared her mind, and the brisk air energized her. She excused her disobedience, believing she would be in much better spirits when the guests arrived.

The higher obstacle ahead appeared daunting as she raced towards it. Ignoring an inner voice of caution, she brought Cinnamon into a gallop. As they approached the jump, she felt Cinnamon shorten her stride, her back rounding. She leaned forward as the horse leaped, then gasped. Cinnamon was not in control!

The horse's back legs kicked off the top rail. Amelia lost her center of balance, slipping far to the side. Cinnamon kept going. She hung on, trying to regain balance.

Suddenly a hand gripped the reins. Another horse sidled up, its rider grasping her arm as Cinnamon slowed and stopped.

"Are you out of your mind?" Lucas jumped off his horse and lifted Amelia as she hung from the saddle. "This horse has no training or conditioning for that rail!" He glared, shaking his head, his jaw clenched. "Are you hurt?"

"I…I am fine. I…"

"If you had slipped any further to the side, you would have fallen and broken bones or gotten trampled."

Amelia opened her mouth to speak but nothing came out. She was shaking and he was right. What had she been thinking?

Lucas must have seen the fear in her eyes. "Let me

get you out of here." Without letting go of his arm around Amelia's waist, he grabbed Cinnamon's reins and led them both through the open gate and to a spectator's bench a few feet away.

His horse obediently followed and began munching on the grass nearby while Lucas tied her horse to a nearby post. Amelia limped to the bench and sat, covering her face in her hands.

"You are injured." He knelt in front of her. "Damn skirts," he muttered as he pulled up the long drape of her riding skirt. "Why women think they can ride like a man wearing a costume that belongs on a stroll in the park, I will never understand." He lifted the ankle she had been rubbing through her boot. With surprising gentleness, he turned her ankle one way and then another, until she squealed. He stopped. "Probably sprained. If I remove your boot, it might swell up and you won't be able to get it back on. The way you twisted in the saddle; I suspect your foot was pushed into an odd angle in the stirrup. You need to stay off it."

"It is only a little sore." Amelia huffed. "I was able to walk this far after you heaved me off my horse."

Lucas smirked. "Heaved? You were ready to fall off," he growled, unceremoniously letting go of her foot before sitting down next to her. "What were you thinking? A horse must have enough muscle strength, coordination, and fitness to jump that high and certainly not with a rider on a side-saddle in a long skirt."

Amelia sighed in defeat and lowered her chin, too humiliated to look at him. She brushed dirt from her skirt. "You have made your point. I should not have attempted it. Cinnamon was doing so well, and I was... well, I overestimated her abilities."

****

One side of Lucas's lips turned up. "Your horse appears fine, and you will be too with some rest on that ankle."

With a finger, he lifted her fallen chin. Big mistake. He gazed into her eyes, so expressive, searching, and moist. She was stubbornly holding back tears. He swept back blonde wisps of hair that had escaped what must have been a neat bun that now hung awkwardly to the side of her hat. His eyes lowered to her lips, slightly raw from the cold. He was fascinated by her slightly quivering bottom lip, causing him to moisten his own. He leaned closer. She did not pull back.

When she bit into her bottom lip, he was lost. Taking a ragged breath, he brought his lips to an inch of hers before catching himself. He pulled back.

"That would not have been very noble, though few expect it of me."

Amelia lifted a finger to her lips. Her gaze fixed on his until she suddenly shook her head as if awakening from a trance. "I need to go." She pushed herself up from the seat. "Ow!"

Lucas jumped up and wrapped an arm around her waist.

"Let me go to Cinnamon." She took a couple of steps.

"I see the way your face is contorting. You are in pain."

Amelia gave a heart-wrenching sigh and gazed at the sky. "I am going to be in so much trouble. Please, if you can help me mount, I should be able to ride."

"You will not make it with that foot. I'll take you

home, and I can return your horse tomorrow."

"No! I mean, I am not even supposed to be out of the house. If my father knew I was here and ..." She paused.

"I understand. This is the last place your father, or your brother, would want you to be without a groom, and with me. Regardless, I am bringing you home. You cannot ride that distance with a sprained ankle." He scratched the stubble on his chin that had grown since his early morning shave, before turning her about to face him. "You appear to be quite good at covert activities. How good are you at sneaking in a back door?"

Wide-eyed, she sucked in her bottom lip, before huffing out a frustrating breath.

"I can pony your horse to mine. Ride with me until we are close to your home. I'll help you mount up then. You can ride the rest of the way. Will your horse be docile enough to allow it?"

"Cinnamon has been ponied in the past but with a skilled rider like my brother."

Lucas laughed. "I assure you I have some proficiency with ponying."

Color rose in her cheeks. "I did not mean to suggest otherwise, Mr. Grey."

"Call me Lucas. After everything we have experienced together, I feel we know each other well enough." He winked. "Sit and rest your ankle. I need to go back to the stable to get a halter rope and a bowline. I'll be right back." He narrowed his eyes. "Do not attempt anything stupid."

****

Amelia opened her mouth to protest, but closed it

and remained still, her hands clasped tightly to her lap as he rode off. Once he was out of sight, she looked about for support until she eyed a stump not far from where her horse was tied.

She stood cautiously, putting mild pressure on the aching ankle as she painfully made her way to Cinnamon. Steadying her stance, she untied her and hopped gingerly over to the stump that was further away than she thought. The ground was soft with wet, fallen leaves that did little to ease the throbbing pain.

When she reached the stump, she tried to position the horse. Instead, she stumbled on the uneven ground. She tried to right herself, only to slip on the wet leaves, her ankle twisting beneath her. Pain shot up her leg. Gritting her teeth, she tried to pull herself up, only to slip again and land on her backside.

"Now I've done it!" She brushed at the soiled arms of her jacket and before glaring down at her muddied riding skirt.

Cinnamon snorted and stepped away.

"Not you too!"

How did she get herself into this mess? She swiped away tears with her stained riding gloves and shivered. The wind was picking up, the sky darkening and she was sitting in the muck. It could not get any worse.

"Oh, but it could." She sobbed.

How was she to enter the house looking like this? And what if someone sees her with Grey? And where is he? She did not have to wonder for long. She groaned at the look Lucas gave her when he rode up and spotted her on the ground.

"Could you be any more pig-headed?" He jumped from his horse and lifted her off the ground by her armpits. "What am I to do with you?"

His heaving breath caressed her cheeks as he lifted her onto his horse.

"Hold on and stay put."

Amelia dared not say a word. With a lead rope and reins, Lucas positioned Cinnamon to the right of his horse and mounted behind Amelia.

"Wrap your arms around my waist and hold on tight." After grabbing his reins in his left hand, he transferred Cinnamon's lead rope to his right. "We ride slow until your horse gets comfortable. Mine is accustomed to ponying, but I do not usually have an innocent in my arms while I ride."

Amelia obeyed, afraid to speak. There was nothing she could say to make it better.

He pulled at the ribbons that held her hat and tugged them down. "Sorry, but they are in my face. Lower your head."

Amelia rested her cheek on his chest, now muddied from rescuing her. Her embarrassment was replaced by the realization of his warm body resting against hers. She had never been this close to a man.

They rode away from the stables and onto the road before Lucas spoke.

"By the way, Lady Pierce, the mistake you made when trying to jump that rail was leaning forward. I would be happy to give you some lessons. That is if you can return."

"I may never be able to leave the house again."

"I shall miss you then," Lucas whispered, close to her ear.

Her heart swelled at his words despite her fear mingled with disbelief that this was happening. She had been certain he saw her as a fool, spoiled, and reckless. *He will miss me?*

The air grew colder by the time they reached the border of her father's land.

"There is a path over to the right that leads to the back gardens," she said as her anxiety grew.

Her cheek brushed his chin when she lifted her head to point. She was startled at its roughness and caught his gaze. He wore a rakish grin. Mortified, she lowered her gaze. His arm tightened around her. As they grew closer to the house, the lanterns were already lit near the stables. To her relief, no one was about. Would her luck hold out?

"Please, stop now, before we reach the clearing. I can take Cinnamon to the stables from here. There should be a groom about who can help me."

"You can barely walk, and I doubt you can ride either."

"I must. I can walk. Please, I beg you not to go any further. For your own sake as well as mine."

He dismounted, released the ties on Cinnamon. and reached for her. His hands remained on her waist as he brought her to the ground, his face lowering to hers, only inches away, until he slowly released his hold.

"Walk slowly, leaning on your horse. Keep as much weight as you can off that ankle. Perhaps your injury might draw mercy for your rebellion." His last comment sounded almost scornful, his lips tightening before he shrugged and turned away.

Amelia felt suddenly as if she'd been a burden he was happy to be rid of.

She straightened her hat and jacket. "I have taken you from your duties at the stables. I should apologize to Mr. Winston." Amelia realized she sounded condescending and took a breath. "I do appreciate your aid, Mr. Grey. I would have been in quite a fix if you hadn't helped me. I do not know how to thank you."

"I shall think of something." He gave her a teasing grin and handed her Cinnamon's reins before mounting his horse.

She nodded and limped down the wooded path and into the yard. Daring to look back, she saw that he remained where she'd left him, watching her. Her ankle throbbed, but it was the least of her worries.

Her mind was in a dither of calamitous thoughts. She might be able to accept any disciplinary measures for riding out alone, but her shock over another awkward experience with Lucas Grey would be harder to overcome. He had saved her from worse injury after her foolish attempt at jumping that hurdle. Despite calling her pigheaded and scolding her, he demonstrated a kindness she never would have expected from him. Even more alarming was the heightening of all her senses as she sat clutching his jacket during the ride home. She remembered his heated breath on her cheeks and the motion of his body moving with hers.

She needed to stop her wayward thoughts. He was simply being kind once again. She shouldn't make any more of the situation. Grey had come to her aid, no less than anyone else would have done at the arena. Using Cinnamon as a support, she limped the remaining way to the open doors of the stable,

Albert was the groom on hand. He often accompanied her on her rides and was quite willing to while away time under a shade tree while she galloped across fields in his view. A few times when she returned nearly half an hour later, she would find him asleep. They both kept their disobedience to themselves and today, she depended on his aid and his discretion.

He rushed over. His eyes widened at her appearance. "Milady, what happened?'

"I had a fall, but I am quite all right."

He narrowed his eyes before taking Cinnamon's reins. "I'll get your horse taken care of, but first, allow me to escort you back to the house."

"Thank you, Albert. I could use your arm for support, but I prefer to use the back entrance." She was thankful he asked no questions.

To her good fortune, no one saw her limping up the back stairs. She slipped into her room, closed the door, and sank into a chair. Before she could breathe a sigh of relief at making it to her room unnoticed, she gazed down at the encrusted mud on her boots. Had she left a path of grime along the way?

She dropped her face in her hands, trying to hold back a sob at the mess she'd made, not the dirt on her skirt, but humiliation and a plethora of feelings she feared to analyze. Weeping now would not help.

Amelia considered her dilemma and decided a partial truth was best. She had simply gone off on a short ride without a groom and attempted to jump over a fallen log. She lost her balance and twisted her ankle in the stirrup. Father would be furious that she did not call for a groom to accompany her, but his anger was better than learning the truth and who brought her home.

She would accept her father's rage at her disobedience and apologize to the maids for giving them more to do. With guests arriving in a few days, they were already overworked. Her rebellion was not only at her own cost, and she felt terrible about it. She nearly jumped from her seat at the sudden knock at the door.

"Lady Amelia, may I come in?"

Amelia started to rise but slumped back. "Come in, Edith."

Her maid entered, wagging a finger. "Best let me see what you have done. Albert sought me out. When I came up an hour ago and saw you were not here and your bed untouched, I suspected you had gone off. Little is kept from the servants, milady. Do you think I am unaware of your occasional escapes?"

"Oh, Edith. I suppose I have not been as discreet as I thought."

"Fortunately, your father has too much on his mind to notice your disappearances."

"You have covered for me before then."

"You have not made it easy, and I do want to keep my position."

"I am sorry, and grateful too."

Edith sighed before looking her up and down. "Aren't you a sight? We must get you out of those clothes and get them cleaned. It will be as if you never left. Albert told me you were limping badly. He also said he was riding behind you when your horse sidestepped to avoid a rabbit and you nearly fell."

"He did?"

She had hinted to Albert that his discretion about her riding out alone was appreciated. He must have felt the need to cover for her with a tale.

"That is what he told me to say if your father asks.

Now I need to remove your boots so I can take a look at that ankle."

****

An hour later, bathed, in her nightgown, and with her ankle wrapped and lifted on a cushion, she sat up in her bed, staring out her window into the dark. Edith had brought her dinner after telling her father she was not feeling well. Thankfully, he took the news without asking questions. Tomorrow morning, she would have to embellish Albert's story. She felt guilty that the servants were party to her deceptions, but, thankfully, no one knew the true cause of her injury, except Lucas Grey.

Amelia touched a finger to her lips, remembering the moment Lucas, the illegitimate son of the Duke of Radford, came close to kissing her. Had she imagined it? Her aunt had told her of his reputation as a rake, but she did not sense that he was taking advantage. He went out of his way to help her. Even with his arm snug around her waist on the ride home, he had remained a gentleman. He could have taken advantage, but she arrived home safely.

The situation could have been a nightmare if anyone had seen them. What if he had not come to her rescue? She shuddered at the thought of what would have happened to her.

She wondered what might be going through his mind. Remembering his closeness, an embarrassing pleasure kept her reliving moments for some time before she finally fell asleep.

Chapter 11

"You have not explained to my satisfaction how you took that nasty spill on your horse," Eva said as she sat on the edge of her sister's bed, fluffing the cream-colored lace that fringed the puff sleeves of her violet crepe gown.

Amelia stood nearby, staring into her looking glass. "I would rather not talk about it." As she pinned back a stray tendril that had escaped her tightly wound chignon, she remembered when Lucas's fingers swept strands of hair away from her face. Why could she not stop thinking of him? "I like the deeper rose design on the bodice and sleeves, but I rather think the flowers on the hem could have been omitted. Aunt Libby and her *modiste* insisted they were a nice finish."

"I like the gown just as the *modiste* designed it, and all the floral accents bring out the lighter rose of the gown. You are purposely changing the subject. I cannot imagine how you were able to right yourself without a groom's aid."

"My horse is quite patient with me." Amelia eyed her sister through the mirror and observed her doubtful expression. She refused to admit, even to Eva, her closest confidant, how and where the accident occurred. She wished she hadn't confessed that she had gone out without a chaperone. "A week has passed and my ankle has healed. I prefer not to dwell on the incident."

Straightening her pearl necklace and with a swish of her skirt, she turned to face her sister. "Our guests must be wondering about our absence."

"I suppose we should return," Eva agreed with little enthusiasm. "No doubt the men are still off playing cards. We needed to escape Lady Hastings's blathering. I could not bear one more of her long-winded tales. If she is still dominating the conversation, I might feign a faint."

"At least you can return home. I am her captive. She has an endless store of London gossip. I'm surprised she stops talking long enough to hear the stories she passes on."

Eva rose from the bed and checked her appearance in the mirror. "I suspect Lenora adds colorful beads of detail to draw in her listeners. I question how much of her rambling to believe. Is she staying through to the New Year?"

"No, but we have the pleasure of her company for a few more days. She's going to her daughter's home for a short visit and plans to return for the ball. I can bear her for a bit longer. It is Lord Blakely who I wish would carry his irksome flirtations off to anywhere else but here."

"The viscount has taken quite a liking to you, Amelia. He is not unattractive although he has grown soft in the gut since the last time I saw him."

"If his sire was not one of our father's dearest friends, I would beg to have him tossed out on his rear. You must save me when he insists on being my partner in the parlor games."

"I shall do my best, but Drake and I shall be leaving soon to see his family." Eva reached for her sister's hand. "You have orchestrated everything so beautifully for the guests. Mother would be proud."

"Thank you." Amelia smiled and gave a soft squeeze to her sister's hand before opening her bedroom door. "Come, we must join the ladies."

"Perhaps we can urge Aunt Libby to snatch you away from Blakely's advances," Eva said quietly as she and Amelia descended the staircase.

When they reached the parlor, they saw most of the women had retired, including Lenora Hastings.

"It appears we stayed away long enough," Amelia whispered.

"Or they are off to another room gossiping about the present company," Eva said, a hand covering her mouth before they strolled arm in arm toward the small gathering that remained.

While Eva joined the women who sat together in a corner of the room, Amelia approached Aunt Libby who stood alone by the hearth, gazing into the fire.

"You appear to be in deep reflection, both in thought and in the light of the flame," she said with a smile before observing her aunt's disturbed expression. "Is something wrong?"

"Better not to speak of it now," Libby murmured. Her gaze darted toward the other women. "I am going upstairs. You need to be gracious to your guests. After they retire, come to my room." She left without another word.

Pressing a knuckle to her chin, she paused, wondering what could be wrong. Her aunt was obviously disturbed about something.

An hour later, she entered her aunt's bedroom and found her changed into a flannel nightgown, wrapped in a shawl and sitting in her rocking chair. Her white hair, no longer in a bun, was brushed out as was her custom, but her face was drained of color.

"Aunt Libby, are you ill?"

"Only ill at heart."

Amelia sat on the velvet-cushioned window seat nearby. "What has upset you so?"

Libby exhaled a deep sigh. "Your ring, my dear, has been found."

Amelia blinked in surprise. She gripped the edge of the soft cushion and leaned toward her aunt. "Where? When did you hear of this?"

"Your father called me to his study while you were in your room with your sister. If there hadn't been guests, he would have sent for you."

Libby's shoulders sagged back in the chair as if the meeting with her brother had been not only troubling but exhausting. Her gaze lowered to the handkerchief she held in her hands. It was crumpled and twisted to a quarter of its size. Libby flattened the piece of cotton in her lap and refolded it, before looking up.

"Expect to be summoned in the morning. Your father was enraged by the details. I can only hope that his temper will have cooled by then."

"Enraged? But why?" She caught herself at the weariness on her aunt's face. "I am sorry that you have been drawn in again. Father has upset you. Why must he ruin your evening? Certainly, I am curious how it was found. His men searched the stable floor a fortnight ago without finding it. Someone must have discovered it since. Did a messenger arrive with it in hand?" Secretly she wondered if Lucas had been the one to find it. She was struck suddenly by her aunt's words. "You say he was enraged over the details. What do you mean? Who found my ring?"

"Lord Frederick Blakely has it in his possession."

"The viscount?" Amelia gaped at her aunt who gave a confirming nod. She rose from her seat and paced in a circle, biting down on a knuckle, before collapsing back. "How can that be?"

"Are you prepared to hear the details? I grant you they will be upsetting, but best you hear them from me before you face your father. During their game of faro, Blakely bragged about winning a valuable emerald ring in a poker game in London. Your brother asked for a description, which left him no doubt it was the ancestral ring you wore."

"In London?" Amelia's jaw dropped. Questions and suspicions crowded into her thoughts.

"Yes. Roderick asked him who gambled it away. According to your brother, Blakely, quite in his cups, could not remember the name of the 'fool', as he put it. He did remember the man saying his stepbrother with 'tainted royal blood' had found the ring."

Amelia looked away from her aunt, struggling with the implication.

"The player, according to the viscount, was so sure of his poker hand, he boasted the winnings on the table were more than a merchant would pay. He threw the ring into the pot. Blakely had a better hand."

A stab of pain cut into Amelia's heart. "Grey found it," she murmured.

She didn't want to believe what she was hearing, but it must be true. Images of him searching with her, coming to her rescue at the track, his look of concern, all of it flashed through her mind. Indeed, the memories filled her secret thoughts.

"When we saw Lucas Grey in London," Libby continued, "I overheard him say he was staying with his stepbrother. He must have found it and given him the ring to sell."

Anger replaced Amelia's shock, swelling from the pit of her stomach to her throat.

"There is more you should know." Her aunt heaved a heavy sigh. "Blakely believes his generosity to return the ring should be compensated. He desires to court you and has asked for your father's blessing. Your father is furious. He may very well betroth you to him."

"Never! He is an insufferable braggart and a pest." Amelia pushed herself off the seat again and stalked back and forth in the small room.

"Keep your voice down, dear, before you wake the house. I must warn you, your father plans to send for the constable in the morning and have Grey arrested."

Amelia sunk onto the corner of her aunt's bed and covered her face with her hands. She had been the fool.

"There is nothing more to be said tonight, and I am tired," Libby said, stifling a yawn. "Daylight will bring trouble of its own."

Her actions were the cause of all of it. "I am sorry you have been drawn into this fiasco. I pray you will sleep well."

She kissed her aunt's cheek and left the room, holding back tears until she closed her own bedroom door. Lying on her bed she sobbed tears of rage and tears for her foolishness in giving a deceitful tyrant a place in her heart.

****

She woke with a start at the sound of her name.

Her ring, Lucas. All returned in an instant.

"Milady, you must wake up," Edith said, drawing open the bedroom curtains. "Why, you are still in your gown from last evening. Were you so exhausted?"

Dragging herself to a sitting position, she looked out the windows at the gray, gloomy morning, not unlike her mood.

"You look as if you barely slept, and your hair! We must brush it out and get you properly dressed. Your father has requested your presence in his study."

Oh, no. Amelia rubbed her eyes as her aunt's words from the night before flooded into her consciousness. "What time is it?"

"Just past seven, miss. Your father wants to see you before the guests rise for the day."

Her mind was as cloudy as the weather. She pushed herself off the bed and allowed Edith to help her out of her gown and pull out the pins in her hair. Once her toilette was complete, she was as prepared as she could be to see her father. Thanking Edith, she left the room. She was not prepared to face Lenora Hastings who scurried toward her from the end of the hall, like a pup eager for a snack. Had the woman been waiting for her to appear?

"Good morning, Amelia," she said in a raised whisper, her expression too exuberant for the time of day. "I am an early riser myself. I adore the early morning. Those who sleep until noon, miss the best part of the day. Don't you agree?"

Before Amelia could step away, Lenora curled her arm around hers and drew her snug against her bony side. She was still in her robe, her hair tied back, and her lined, narrow face, pale without the excessive makeup she usually wore.

"I know I must appear a sight." Lenora patted her graying hair. "I peered out of my room when I heard footsteps in the hall. When I saw your maid enter your room. I thought… Indeed, I almost knocked on your door. I feared I would disturb you, but I felt certain you would want to hear the news before it becomes common knowledge."

"What is it?"

Lenora drew her face closer and whispered. "I awakened out of a sound sleep way past midnight. You know how the men play their card games through the night. My husband came in and told me about Lord Blakely's admission and the furor it caused at the table from your brother. I wanted to prepare you before others spoke out of turn." Lenora paused, her brows raised as if waiting for Amelia to indulge her with either confirmation of the news or surprise at the telling.

Amelia wanted to turn her back on the woman; but she was a guest, therefore, deserved civility. She would not give her the pleasure of an emotional reaction. "Yes, I have heard. If you will excuse me." She tried to step away only to have the woman clasp her arm more firmly.

"I was unaware that you lost a valuable ring. Indeed, what a scandal to have of all men, the Duke of Radford's ill-conceived son involved in its disappearance."

Amelia gaped, realizing that more had been revealed around the card table than news of her ring being discovered.

"Oh dear, you have not been fully informed.

Indeed, it is too early. You must have been heartbroken to have lost such a treasure. Take comfort that your precious ring has been recovered and shall be returned. I do wonder how you lost such a treasure and how it could get into the hands of Radford's bastard." Lenora paused.

"I really must see to today's schedule." She used her free hand to unhook the woman's hold on her arm. "Enjoy your day, Lenora."

She descended the staircase, her head high, and with more grit than grace. Lenora's insufferable nosiness had succeeded in reminding her of the truth she had faced once her tears were spent.

She had fantasized about falling in love with Lucas Grey. She'd believed he was caring and honorable and did not deserve to be scorned for no other reason than his ignoble birth. She even imagined ways she could sneak off to see him. How naïve she had been. He wore a fake façade of helpfulness and concern while knowing he'd found and kept her ring. She had been drawn in like a fly to a spider's web, but he was going to be snared instead.

She marched toward her father's study, ready to encourage him to call in the constable.

****

"How difficult this day must have been for you," Aunt Libby said to Amelia when she and Eva joined her in her private sitting room later in the afternoon.

The other women had gone to their rooms after enjoying an outing to collect holiday greenery. Eva and her husband Drake had returned from visiting his family that morning. While Drake joined the men for target shooting, Amelia caught her sister up with the news.

"The day was tiring, but I am the hostess as Father felt the need to remind me of this morning."

"He appears to have risen above the incident, at least for his guests," Libby said. "No doubt he was stewing beneath his lordly exterior. You cloaked your anxiety well, though I could see a sadness in your eyes.

"I hope I was not as transparent to our guests," Amelia said, stifling a yawn as she gazed at the flickering candle by her chair.

"You were especially gracious, despite the murmuring and raised brows among some of the guests," her sister added. "A few take great pleasure from another's calamity. Your disinterest in adding to their need for drama must have disappointed them, especially Lady Hastings and her retinue. Unfortunately, the news of Duke of Radford's bastard son's involvement gave them enough dirt to dig and some scintillating sighs to smother beneath their haughty exterior."

Amelia's focus returned as she cocked her head toward her sister. "What are you talking about?"

"I thought that might draw you out of your lethargy," Eva said, with a teasing grin. "After discussing Lucas Grey's appalling offense against you in their lofty tones of abhorrence, the gaggle's conversation brought stifled gasps and giggles."

"It appears I missed out on that particular conversation." Aunt Libby sat beside Eva on the brocade settee, knitting."

"You left to accompany Lady Catherine and her mother to the orangery to view the winter garden collection of tropical fruits and greenery. Amelia was in the kitchen checking on the dinner preparations when Catherine's name was linked to Grey's. I did not believe either of you would be surprised."

"It's no secret that a few of the wives of our peers indulge in liaisons, Lady Catherine among them. She is over twenty years younger than her husband. Not to excuse her behavior, but he has had his mistresses over the years. I hardly think he can please them in bed at his age, but his pockets can satisfy." Libby snorted.

"Grey deserves his reputation in that regard," Eva said. "One of the lady's comments about a 'delicious encounter' brought a round of giggles."

"They will not be able to partake in another delicious encounter when he is behind bars," Amelia said, still staring at the flickering candle.

"Do you want to tell us about your meeting with Father this morning?" Eva asked.

"The meeting with Father or the discreet visit from the constable? I doubt our guests were left unaware. They would have expected him to act on the news."

"I hope my brother did not take his anger out on you. You simply lost a ring. You are not responsible for Mr. Grey's pilfering."

"No, Roderick was more concerned Blakely's drunken admission would mar our visitors' stay. He had little regard for Grey, to begin with, especially after Roderick's telling of the stable incident." Amelia grimaced. "Since no gossip came forth in that regard, he was glad the ring would be returned and 'Radford's bastard' arrested."

"What of Blakely's request for recompense?" Aunt Libby asked.

"The audacity of the buffoon." Eva huffed.

"Father told me about his insane request. He is aware of the viscount's self-indulgent nature. In his words, he would prefer to marry me off to someone else, but if I insist on begging off from every man who desires to court me, he shall have no choice but to choose my husband. At least he wants better for me than Blakely."

"Well then, what caused the half-hearted smiles and gloom today?" Eva asked. "At one point, you appeared on the precipice of tears before collecting yourself when duty called."

"I slept little after hearing the news. I was tired and, I suppose, embarrassed about the entire debacle."

Both her sister and her aunt did not know the truth about her injured ankle and Lucas's part in it. Her poor judgment of his character and her foolish imagining were hers to keep locked in her heart.

"We have a long night ahead. We should prepare for the dinner hour. I expect my mood will lighten with some needed rest."

Amelia chose not to add that news of Grey's forthcoming arrest might be even more satisfying than a good night's sleep.

Chapter 12

Lucas wiped the sweat from his brow and contemplated what still needed to be done. He and Tom had worked all morning, checking the footings on the perimeter of the property. He recorded those that needed repair before the harsher weather set in and others that needed to be checked again in the spring. They both stopped abruptly when Otis, one of Winston's grooms, rode up in a fast gallop.

"Grey, Winston wants you in his office," Otis said, breathing heavily.

"Nearly done here. Just need half an hour. Did it appear urgent?"

"Looks like trouble brewing from the looks of it."

Surprised by the summons and the severe expression on Otis's face, Lucas tossed a tool in a nearby satchel and brushed the dirt off his trousers. Rather than question Otis further, he'd best check the matter himself. "Tom, take a break. We can finish up this afternoon."

When he arrived at Winston's office near the entrance to the main arena, he noticed three horses tied to the rail. Winston had visitors.

Constable Withers, a short, plump, grizzly bearded man who wore a perpetual scowl, looked Lucas up and down when he walked into the office. Lucas called in the constable on rare occasions when a soused customer caused a ruckus and needed a night in jail. Without a crowd about, there was no reason for his visit.

A man he didn't recognize stood next to Withers. He had the opposite appearance, tall and reed-thin, with a dusty brown beard narrowed to a point below his chin. He stood with his arms crossed and his lips curled as if he were both pleased and ready for action.

Winston spoke up just as the constable stepped forward. "Lucas, Constable Withers tells me there is an accusation against you."

Lucas narrowed questioning eyes at Winston before glaring at the constable. "An accusation?"

"Theft, Mr. Grey, of a valuable emerald ring. The Earl of Weatherly is your accuser. Winston has assured us of your cooperation."

"Lucas, do you deny the charge?" Winston, sitting at his desk, hunched forward. His white eyebrows arched as he waited for an explanation.

The ring. Thoughts swirled through Lucas's mind before meeting Wither's icy stare. "I don't understand the charge."

"I assure you I will investigate thoroughly. Meanwhile, you must come with us. His gaze darted to his partner. "Malcolm can be overly persuasive if you choose otherwise."

When the taller man took an aggressive step toward him, Lucas held his ground, sneering at Wither's lackey before answering. "Weatherly's daughter lost that ring in the stables during one of the arena events. There was no theft."

Taking the ring to London and his brother's actions surfaced. The memory remained like a brick in his chest.

"Do you deny offering Lady Amelia Pierce, Weatherly's daughter, a hand in searching for the ring?" Withers asked in his most formidable tone.

"Yes, I offered to help her."

"And it was not found during the search?"

"No." His gaze remained steady on the constable.

"You have nothing more to add?"

"I did not steal the lady's ring."

"Grey has demonstrated reliability and trustworthiness in my employ. Do you have any other proof he committed a crime?" Winston asked in his usual calm, restrained voice.

Lucas swallowed hard at his words. He hated that the man he admired more than any other had become involved. The thought of losing his respect left a hollow in his throat.

Withers turned a suspicious gaze from Lucas to Winston. "Mr. Grey was in London on business for you a fortnight ago?"

"Yes." Winston's brow furrowed. "I was ailing. Lucas took care of some business for me. He was gone only a few days."

"During that time, the valuable ring Lady Pierce lost was wagered in a poker game in London. The man who won the jewel plans to return it to its rightful owner. I cannot say more until I have statements from others involved." Withers turned back to Lucas. "If you have nothing more to add, perhaps a few days in jail might improve your memory."

"Lucas?" Winston urged.

Lucas pressed his lips together. He refused to look back at Winston as Malcolm took his arm and led him out.

The ride to the local jail was slow, leaving him time to think. If he told the whole story, he would be accusing his stepbrother of theft. Graham did not deserve his loyalty and silence, but he was the one who brought the ring to London. Would they believe he meant to return it? Would Graham be charged and imprisoned? They might both be incarcerated.

So much remained undone at the stables. With no opportunity to leave instructions, little would get done. If he could not prove his innocence, the future he had worked so hard for would fade as quickly as the morning mist. To the peers of the realm, he was no more than a bastard and his stepbrother, a schemer. If the earl has his way, he and Graham could be imprisoned without a morsel of mercy.

****

Little could be done over the weekend for the investigation. Sleeping on straw was not new to Lucas. He had spent nights on a hayed floor waiting for the birth of a colt, but the cell Withers caged him in smelled of dampness, filth, and mold. He accepted water from the jailer, but he had no appetite for the stale bread or rancid cheese offered.

Rage ate at his insides, both at Graham and at himself, but the visit from his mother on Sunday morning brought him shame. When she stood before him, the bars between them, the jailer stepped away, allowing them a few minutes alone. Her eyes filled as she took in his appearance. She wiped at them and bit down on her lips before speaking.

"Oh, Lucas, how did this come about?"

"You should not be here, Mother. How did you find out? And how did you get here?"

"John Winston came to the door himself to tell me. Iris heard it later from a neighbor. Gossip carries faster than leaves in the wind, my son. Mr. Winston offered to have one of his men drive me to see you. Iris accompanied me. She is waiting outside. Lucas, I refuse to believe the charge against you."

He winced at seeing the dark circles beneath his mother's eyes, and the fear on her face. "I assure you I did not steal the ring. Complications arose, difficult to explain. The ring was lost, not stolen. Let me work this out."

"What can I do to help? I brought food and a change of clothes." She gazed over to the jailer, who nodded.

"Please, take care of yourself. I appreciate what you brought, but there is nothing else you can do. Go home and get some rest."

The jailer stepped toward them. Her time was up.

Georgetta put her hand through the bars as she smoothed Lucas's unshaven cheek. "I believe you," she whispered. "I shall pray."

Lucas glared at the door as she was led out until it slammed shut behind her. He gripped the bars and cursed.

****

Constable Withers appeared at his cell Tuesday morning wearing an arrogant grin. "Grey, I hope you're finding your accommodations bearable. You have had a few days to dwell on the situation while I have been busy conducting the investigation. Are you prepared to talk, or do you still proclaim your innocence?"

Lucas had prepared his statement. Keeping his anger under control at the smirk on the constable's face took greater effort.

"Lady Pierce lost the ring when she pulled off a glove while caring for her horse in the main stable. I offered to help her search. Her brother is a witness as well to the incident. You must admit it is impossible to steal a lost item. I have nothing more to say."

In the hours he'd spent on the floor of the cell, he realized if the court was fair, they could not prove he had stolen Amelia Pierce's ring. She had admitted the loss. One of her father's men could have found it during their search. How could they prove otherwise?

Withers rubbed his grizzled beard. "I had hoped the days spent here might loosen your tongue. Regardless, this will be a busy day. John Winston has requested a visit with you. He should arrive within the hour. I have also located your stepbrother, Graham Montrose."

Lucas's facial muscles tensed as he glared down at the short, round-bellied constable.

"After much hesitance, your stepbrother admitted he'd had possession of the jewel in question and wagered it. According to Lord Frederick Blakely, who won it from him in a poker game, Montrose was quite drunk. Blakely related that your stepbrother slobbered on about his brother, who had 'the blood of a duke in his veins but without the honor', had acquired the ring. Who else could he be talking about, Mr. Grey? Unfortunately, Montrose refused to say more. He is being brought here this afternoon to join you until the investigation is complete. You will both be brought before the chief magistrate later this week. Perhaps, Montrose may be more forthcoming with information when he sees you with a four days' growth of a beard and straw stuck to your hair and trousers." Withers grinned. "I will leave you to your thoughts."

Lucas gritted his teeth as the man waddled out. He combed his fingers through knotted hair. What else did Graham reveal? He slid down against the gray walls of the cell. Lowering his head, he sat with his arms folded across his bent knees.

Winston was coming to see him. What could that mean?" He rose and paced the small cell.

The hour seemed endless. Winston should be here soon. With hunched shoulders, he pressed his back against the bars and fisted his hands in his pockets before squinting at his wrinkled trousers. Nothing could be done about his appearance and his need for a shave and a steaming hot bath. Difficult and grueling work at the stables often left him grimy, but it had purpose. Having John Winston visit him in a damp, dingy cell was more than humiliating.

He admired John and worked diligently to earn the older man's trust. Winston Stables was more than a livelihood or a place to spend his days. He toiled with enthusiasm and grit not only for personal gain. He wanted to ease John's workload. Much work must be completed now that the equestrian competitions were over. Winter storage, repairs, orders, the list was long, and John's health was failing of late. Winston counted on him to keep the place running smoothly and profitably.

Lucas swore under his breath. The sound of a door shoved open drew him from his dismal thoughts. In moments, John Winston approached the cell, his weather-worn face appeared older and wearier than it had in his office days earlier.

How many days was it? Lucas had lost count.

Winston acknowledged him with a grim nod, saying nothing until the jailer left them alone, but not out of sight.

"Are you well?"

"As well as can be expected in my present accommodations." He gave a rueful grin. "I am deeply sorry you have become involved in this situation. You shouldn't be here, John. I'll work this out soon."

"I have been given only a few minutes to speak with you." Winston inhaled a deep breath, before gazing directly into Lucas's eyes. "With deep regret, I have no choice but to relieve you of your position at the stables, at least for the time being."

"Lucas reeled for a split second before grasping the bars. True, he'd barely eaten that morning and little the days before. And the news wasn't unexpected. He thought he was prepared, but his worst fears had materialized. He took a breath before straightening his stance.

"I understand, John."

He could not hold a grudge against him for his decision.

"Unfortunately, I have been approached by more than one important customer, participant, and wealthy contributor to the events. They threaten to remove their business and their horses from Winston Stables if I allow you to stay. I have little understanding of the charge, and believe you are innocent of thievery. He lowered his eyes and gave a dismal shake of his head. "I cannot afford to lose the business. I am too old to begin again."

Lucas nodded. He understood the business too well. Winston had no choice.

The jailer's shuffling footsteps and raspy cough sent a message that Winston's time was up."

"John, I realize your position. I appreciate that you were gracious enough to come here and sorry you had to do so." He wanted to say more, but it wasn't the time. He gave an accepting nod and offered a half-smile.

Winston opened his mouth as if he wanted to say more. Pressing his lips together, he turned and followed the jailer out.

Lucas remained at the bars, gazing blankly at the wall before him. With a dismal shrug, he stretched out on the layer of straw laid over the stone floor and closed his eyes.

Chapter 13

Amelia gazed through the open doors of the large drawing-room as servants moved furniture to prepare for the holiday ball only two days away. She had been most excited about planning the gala in which her mother had taken such pride. Returning from London early turned out to be beneficial for preparations, yet the embarrassment she had caused her aunt at Lucas Grey's appearance still plagued her. Her gullibility and irrational infatuation for him cast a gloomy cloud over everything. Planning the ball, as well as the daily activities for the guests, helped to keep her from dwelling on Gray and her father's determination to keep him imprisoned.

Knowing he had found the ring and failed to return it infuriated her, but he hadn't stolen it from her possession. He didn't deserve imprisonment. She couldn't forget how he'd helped her. Let his find be his payment. If she could only tell her father how he had rescued her from a worse injury, perhaps he'd see it that way. She couldn't breathe a word of it, especially their intimacy riding home on his horse. She could only imagine her father questioning if anyone saw them. Grey might receive a worse punishment, even a duel.

She needed to be done with the self-reproach. Too much required her attention. This morning her maid, aware Amelia paid more attention to activities than wardrobe, had urged her to choose her gown and accouterments for the ball. She chose the moss green muslin woven with gilt threads that Aunt Libby had insisted upon in London. She remembered her aunt cooing over the fabric, saying how it would highlight Amelia's blonde curls and sparkle in the candlelight. Amelia smiled at the thought. The gown was her favorite. Now that her wardrobe was set, Edith could begin pressing and preparing to make her the belle of the holiday ball, as her maid insisted, while she focused on other details.

More was expected after the gala and leading up to Christmas Day. She had tenants to visit as well as preparing donations to give to the poor and needy in the village. Food baskets, coins, candles, clothing, hats, mittens for the children, and other necessary items would be delivered during the twelve days after Christmas. Gifts for the staff needed to be wrapped. Indeed, she must keep her mind on these other responsibilities and not on Lucas Grey and the misery she had caused.

As the servants worked, she gazed about the room. The crystal chandeliers sparkled, and the wood floor was polished to a high sheen. Drapes and paintings were decorated with garlands of holly, rosemary, and other greens. The gala would be far from a crush. At most, she expected sixty guests including the musicians. The kitchen staff was busy preparing an abundance of food for dinner to be served later in the evening. Dancing and revelry could last until the early morning hours.

If she could only lift her spirits so that she'd be able to enjoy the days ahead.

She was relieved the remainder of the afternoon would be relatively quiet until the dinner hour. Aunt Libby, Lady Catherine and her mother were upstairs in a sitting room, creating needlework gifts. Her father and his friends had gone off on a final fox hunt before more severe weather arrived. She had returned a half-hour before from an afternoon carriage ride to the village with Lady Sarah Hartmann and her sister Dora. The two women were now resting in their rooms. Amelia found both widows pleasant company when Lady Hastings was not about. Although the two women might enjoy listening to Lenora's gossip, they made no mention of the ring issue, at least in Amelia's presence. Lady Hastings and her husband would be returning soon for the ball and would, no doubt, have more stories to tell.

With a frown, Amelia thought about Lenora's return. She could only imagine how she must have chewed on and added tasty tidbits to Blakely's news and the constable's visit while she was away. By now, Grey's arrest was probably the talk of teas and the tattle in salons from here to London.

In the latest report from the constable, Grey and his stepbrother were both jailed. Her father was gratified. She went from anger to despondency from one moment to another. According to the constable, Grey denied the charge but has offered no further explanation. In Amelia's mind, the story was incomplete and mixed with her memories. Baffling.

From all accounts, he deserved his rakish reputation. Had she been deceived by his attentions? What would stop him from taking advantage when a lucrative opportunity presented itself? Her ring was valuable. He was not of the wealthy class, and it was lost. What did he have to lose if he found it and decided to sell it? His reputation was already in question. Now he was in jail and her father was determined to keep him there for as long as possible.

"Lady Amelia, I have found you without the gaggle of ladies surrounding you," Lord Blakely sputtered, drawing to her side.

She retreated a step, only to back herself against a door jamb. "Good afternoon, Lord Blakely. Have all the men returned from the fox hunt?" She glanced over his short stature and down the hall, hoping a servant was nearby.

"I wish you would call me Frederick. Yes, I found the hunt exhilarating. Our fathers have gone to their rooms to rest. Since I am the lone bachelor, I am delighted to find the most attractive of the ladies alone. Not alone, of course, that would be inappropriate." He gave a slight bow before gazing through the open door to see the servants busy and far enough away not to hear their conversation.

Amelia stepped into the hall. "The weather has been very accommodating for outdoor activities. Thankfully, the snow that threatened has held off," Amelia said, offering a hospitable smile. "I hope you are enjoying your stay. You must excuse me. I was just leaving to check on the kitchen staff for dinner preparations." She tried to take a step around him but he adjusted his stance, blocking her way.

"No doubt your cook has everything well in hand. You have been such a gracious hostess. I look forward to Friday evening. Will you honor me with the first dance?"

Amelia's mouth fell half-open at the request. She

wanted desperately to refuse, but how could she do it politely? "How nice of you to ask but as the hostess, I may be—"

"Lady Amelia, has your father told you one of my servants will be arriving tomorrow morning to deliver your ring?"

"No, I did not hear."

"Your father offered monetary compensation to me, but I refused to accept. I am gratified that I could return such a valuable possession. I desire only the pleasure of a dance."

His expression held more than pleasure. He had expectations and was not to be denied, Amelia realized. "I am thankful my ring will be returned to me, and I shall save the first dance for you."

Blakely grinned. "Might you also grant me the honor of placing your cherished ring on your finger tomorrow evening as well?"

Amelia caught herself from grimacing. Instead, without answering, she offered a placating smile. "Please excuse me. I must see to my staff."

"Of course." He stepped aside.

She hurried down the hall, muttering silently.

The self-gratifying, arrogant man. He wants more than my gratitude!

Chapter 14

"I owe you much," Graham murmured, as he stood outside Lucas's cell. "How do I repay you? Annabel's father would have refused to let me marry his daughter if the truth were told."

Graham hung his head and pressed his forehead to the bars. Only an hour before he was behind them with Lucas. The constable had no reason to hold him. Lucas claimed his stepbrother was innocent, and that his only crime was to gamble away a ring he believed his brother had found. Since he could not be charged for theft, he was free to go.

"Get out of here and go plan your wedding. I have not forgotten how you protected me when your father used me as his punching bag. I owed you. As you have told me often, I was the privileged one to have a good mother, a free education, and a comfortable home." Lucas gave a somber grin. "You, on the other hand, were not dealt a fair hand of cards to choose a better path. I will find out, however, if you refuse to do as I have asked. Admit the truth to your betrothed. If she begs off, you must accept her decision."

"I respect that you want to make an honest man of me. I'll tell her the truth and pray she doesn't go to her father. I shall beg forgiveness for my foolish act and assure her of my desire for her to make me a better man."

Lucas smirked. "I believe you'll use every bit of flattery you possess. Go, marry Miss Annabel and have children. Perhaps her father's religious influence will keep you away from drink and schemes."

Graham nodded. "They cannot hold you much longer, Luc. If it were not that your accuser is an earl, you wouldn't be here."

"The constable knows that. He is bowing to the nobility. Those in power and prestige get their way."

"Weatherly knows his daughter lost the ring. Do you think he is punishing you for the scene in the stable his son observed? With your reputation with the ladies, he might…"

"The jailer is waiting for you to leave. By the way, you smell. Take a bath."

"I thought that stench came from you," Graham chided.

"Leave. I'm tired of your company. I believe you will be a married man the next time we meet."

Graham pressed his hand to Lucas's fisted grip on the bars and trudged away.

Lucas rubbed the overgrowth on his chin and sighed. He didn't tell Graham about Winston's visit. The news would spread soon enough. Members of the nobility and the local gentry's business kept the stables and the arena solvent. Men, who had respected Lucas's expertise and business sense, could no longer trust their property, their horses, and equipment, to a thief. Winston had no choice.

He thought of his mother's second visit, again bringing food and clothing. She could hardly bear seeing her son in a jail cell. He'd observed the worry and despair on her face. His demands that she stay at home could not alter her stubbornness.

She had striven to give him all she was able to give throughout his life, and it hurt her that she couldn't help him now. In London when polite society snubbed her, she held her head high. Even her family that had sent her away admired her. Her parents were both dead now. She had friends in the country, but Lucas knew he was the one person she lived for. He had disappointed her often enough, but this was beyond the pale. Still, she stood by him.

His shame for everything and anything he had done that caused her pain, ate at his insides. His lustful trysts had given him pleasure for a time and satisfied his need to humiliate his father. He'd placed those needs above a moral path that would have honored his mother. Eventually, he'd be released and return home without an occupation and under suspicion. He wanted to be able to support his mother as she grew older. Despite his failings, she would stand by him, and in his depth of conscience, he wanted to make her proud.

All he could see now was a bleak future.

Chapter 15

Amelia rose at dawn on Friday after a restless night. She wanted some quiet time this morning. Once the guests rose to break their fast and move about the estate, she would have no time alone. Tonight was the ball. She'd spend a good part of the day seeing that final preparations were going smoothly.

Remembering that Lady Lenora Hastings would also be arriving today brought a groan. Thankfully, most of the guests were leaving before Christmas Day to visit their families.

She thought of her mother's pleasure when all her fastidious planning and preparation created the perfect gala. Would she be pleased with her daughter's first attempt? She wondered if her mother's mind had been clouded with other concerns. She'd always appeared so calm. In Amelia's youthfulness, she had never noticed if her mother felt any turmoil. It could not have always been easy.

In all honesty, she was tired of smiling and pretending all was well in front of their guests.

Her father remained pleased Grey was still in jail, while she struggled with feelings that left her puzzled and depressed. Why would he give her ring to his stepbrother, only to have him lose it in a game of chance? If he had not captured her heart and she had to admit he did, only the loss of the ring would have remained a regret. Her obsessive thoughts of him and his deception could not be put to rest. Nothing made sense, and she was determined to get better answers, but when?

She considered going to see Lucas in jail. She wanted to confront him, to hear from his lips that he found the ring and kept it from her. Maybe then she could stop ruminating about the entire affair. There was no way she could get away without being noticed or questioned. Their guests filled every moment most days, allowing her only an hour or two to rest in the late afternoon.

As she walked through the main part of the house, checking the window displays of holiday greenery, she spotted a carriage enter the grand circular drive. Odd. The early morning mist still hung heavy in the air.

The butler appeared before she could ring for him.

"Bidwell, is Father expecting someone?" she asked, peering out the window. Her mouth fell open when she recognized the ducal crest on the carriage when it drew to a stop at the front entrance.

Bidwell paused for only a moment. "No, milady, quite unexpected. Your father is dressed and just arrived in the breakfast room." Bidwell straightened his coat and cleared his throat, before heading to the door.

Amelia watched from the window as the Duke of Radford exited the carriage. "Oh, my," she stammered.

Was it about Lucas? Could something have happened to him? Questions wrapped in fear and confusion swept through her mind. She pressed a hand to her chest to calm the rapid beating of her heart. What other reason would cause the duke to arrive at their door just past dawn.

She remained at the window, listening, as the duke was given entrance. With a raised voice, he demanded to see her father. If he was not bearing tragic news, he was being quite rude. She recalled her talk with Aunt Libby about an old grievance her father held toward the duke. She never knew the reasons, but this was far from a cordial visit.

Bidwell, in his usual calm and dignified manner, asked the duke to wait in a nearby drawing-room while he sought out his lord. Amelia was tempted to go in and ask the duke's business, but she doubted her father would be pleased.

Just as she was about to toss aside the fear of her father's wrath and make her presence known to the duke, Bidwell returned. Her father would receive him in his study. As the butler and the duke disappeared down the hall, she wondered what her father was thinking about this unexpected visitor. He had refused to have her present when the constable came to call. She would not be kept in the dark about this visit.

Once the duke was led into the study and Bidwell went off to his duties, Amelia crept to the door Bidwell had shut behind him. With nimble fingers, she opened the door a crack. With the Duke of Radford's voice raised in anger, neither man would have noticed, even if the door had creaked. If only she could see her father's reaction.

"How dare you accuse my son of thievery!"

"Your son? You recognize your illegitimate offspring?" Her father sneered.

She pressed her cheek to the door, her heart in her throat.

"You have concealed him and his mother in a

country cottage for most of his life." Lord Weatherly gave a condescending chortle. "I must admit, Grey refuses to be hidden. He had built himself a decent occupation. Now, he is branded a thief and jobless. You must be utterly humiliated."

Jobless? Amelia covered her mouth to suppress a gasp.

"My pride is not the issue," the duke barked. "You have no case against him. He found a lost ring. Is this ridiculous charge more a way to get back at me after all these years? You have never put aside your grievance. Admit it. Your only cause to punish Lucas is because of Georgetta."

Amelia's chin dropped. Lucas's mother? She drew her ear closer to the opening, thankful the study was in the rear of the house where guests seldom appeared unless invited.

"I am surprised you can recall her name," her father said, using his most arrogant tone. "She was a toy you played with and tossed aside."

"Georgetta and I were in love. You could not stand that she chose me over you."

"I would not marry below my station. I loved her enough not to pursue her favor. You ruined her."

It sounded like her father's fist slammed onto his desk. She clutched her chest at her father's angry confession. Her mind could barely take in what she was hearing. The study was a large room and knowing that his desk did not face the door, she dared to nudge it further open, giving her a narrowed view of Lord Radford facing her father. He stood ramrod straight, his hands fisted to his side, his jawline clenched. His forward gaze confirmed her father was standing now.

"We both loved her, Charles," the duke replied in a restrained tone. "We played together as children, never thinking about class differences. Not until our noble restrictions became real to us. When we both returned from university, you took your position as the heir to your father's title immediately and with great pride. Soon after, you set out to find a bride whom your father would approve. Even at Eton, you were so serious-minded, fixed on your future. I never wanted the dukedom, to my father's chagrin. I wanted..." He paused and lowered his head as if anguish was getting the best of him. After sucking in a deep breath, he raised his chin and continued.

"I wanted to marry Georgetta. Damn, we loved each other. I confronted my parents. I begged them to accept my choice of a bride. My mother was abhorred at the thought I would even suggest marriage to someone, not of our ilk. I still remember my father's threatening words before he marched out of the room. 'You will not disgrace my title by marrying beneath you. Have your fun with her and choose a suitable countess or be disowned.'

"Instead of following their dictates, I tried to talk Georgetta into running away and getting married. Shortly after, my father became gravely ill. I was forced to take on the responsibilities I wanted to run from. Yes," the duke nodded, "On the last night we were together, Georgetta and I consummated our love. We were young and desperate, and, indeed, foolish. We ignored common sense and let our passion have its way. I regret I did not foresee the consequences, but I could never regret being with her."

Amelia held her breath, as his words cut into her

heart. She wondered how her father was reacting to the duke's confession. Her stomach churned with shame at hearing the heartache in his voice; yet she remained at the door unable to leave. After an uncomfortable silence, her father spoke. His tone, to Amelia's ears, was incredulous.

"You were willing to defy your parents' demands? To walk away from your inheritance and your responsibilities?"

Radford nodded. "I was very unlike you, Charles. After taking care of whatever was needed while my father remained ill, I went to see Georgetta. By then, she must have known she was in a family way, though it did not show. She greeted me at the door, but did not invite me in. She told me she had been invited to spend the winter with cousins in the country, and was busy packing. When I tried to talk about our relationship, she called it a mistake and insisted we were not suited for one another. She wished me well and closed the door. I did not see her again until years later."

"She never told you of her condition or asked for financial help?"

"No, and she never asked anything of me. I am not surprised. She was selfless and understood the expectations of the nobility. She would not have wanted to cause a scandal that would affect my family with the king, the courts, or my peers. If she had, I would have stood up to my father. I had no idea where she was. Her family was gracious to my repeated requests but would tell me nothing.

"After Father passed, my mother went on a mission to choose a wife for me since I had no desire to seek one. Miranda appeared to be suitable, and I married her.

The rumors that Georgetta had a child did not reach me until after I succeeded my father, and my wife was heavy with child. At first, I assumed she had married until rumors grew that her son had a strong resemblance to me."

The room went silent again. Had her father noticed the slightly open door? She heard no movement towards the door, and she ignored her conscience telling her to leave. Lord Radford was fighting for his son. She had to hear more.

"Georgetta was the talk of the ton when she returned to London. By then, the child was, perhaps, five years old, and yes, he looked just like you. Georgetta held her head high. I could not fault her. Only you, for ruining her. I cared deeply for her once but, I admit, not with the passion I hear from you. I felt that kind of love for my wife. My father demanded obedience and decorum, but I also wanted the title and everything that went with it." There was no longer arrogance evident in his voice.

Her father's chair was drawn and from the duke's gaze, it appeared he had returned to his seat. The mood of the room had changed dramatically, and her father's voice reflected weariness, and something else. Regret?

"I admit I was envious of the freedom you took advantage of at college, the parties, the sports. Having my father see my high marks and praise me was my focus and what I lived for then." His tone had turned bitter. "Yet, he gave me little praise."

Amelia wiped away a tear. She had never heard such open honesty about her father's past.

"When I heard how Georgetta's ruined reputation was being blathered about because of you, the envy I felt in our college years, turned to hatred. I observed you at affairs and galas with your wife. You were always quiet and aloof. I listened to peers honor you with words to your face, while they snickered behind your back. They would joke about how you were giving your bastard son the best education and supporting your light skirt. I simmered with rage at the names they used for her and blamed you."

The duke's face contorted and he appeared to be staring into space before returning his gaze toward her father's desk. "Charles, I have no excuse for my mistakes and the pain I caused. Blame me, but do not take it out on my son. He is the victim of my indiscretion. Georgetta lives for that young man." He turned toward the window and swept a hand through his silvery hair.

Amelia noticed he looked away from her father when pain over Georgetta Grey bled through his words. She sensed he was sharing feelings he had kept locked away from others.

"When I learned of Lucas's existence, I wanted to see him, but if I could not be a father to him in all ways, I would have hurt him and Georgetta more. I did not belong in their lives. His gaze returned toward her father's direction and his voice hardened. "I was in a marriage with a cold, indifferent wife, who cared little, even for our daughter Stephanie. The most I could offer Georgetta was trivial, the minimal financial support she would accept for her living conditions and a modest home. I insisted on a fine education for Lucas, and she accepted to ensure her son's economic future. Still, it was a pitiable pittance of what I wanted to give her. When my wife passed, it was too late. I keep a distant eye. I know my son despises me. I am disappointed in his rakish behaviors that have come to my ears yet I am proud of his accomplishments."

"He knew it was my daughter's ring. Instead of returning it, he went off to London to sell it."

"Questions have arisen about that assumption. Georgetta came to see me and told me of his imprisonment." A glimmer of a smile appeared on his profile and as quickly disappeared. "She believes in his innocence and has asked me to intervene. Her request is the first time she has asked anything of me."

"How difficult that must have been for her. Not only in the asking, but from what I understand, she carries injuries from the accident that killed her husband."

"Life has never been easy for her," the duke replied, breathing out a heavy sigh. "I beg you, withdraw the charge. I shall find out the truth and will take my son to task for any part of a deception. If you desire payment to rectify the loss, I will gladly give whatever you ask."

Amelia bit her lip at the long pause that ensued. She thought how difficult his visit and his plea must be for the duke.

"The ring, William, a family heirloom passed down from my late wife's mother and grandmother is being returned today. You must have heard that Lord Ellington's son won it from Grey's stepbrother in a poker game. Lord Blakely is here visiting. When he realized it was Amelia's lost ring, he insisted on returning it without compensation. One of his servants will be delivering it today."

Amelia rolled her eyes at his mention of the

viscount. He was a calculating moron. She could not imagine her ring was being returned out of simple courtesy. She started at a shuffling noise. Her father must have risen from his chair. Amelia began to leave, but the duke's next words stopped her.

"My son has lost his position at the stables. That alone is a dire punishment for him. Georgetta told me Lucas was most proud he was able to contribute to their home. He insisted she not accept anything more from me. He wanted to support her fully."

Amelia wished she could see her father's expression. His tone of voice had turned somber and more amiable during the interaction, even calling the duke by his given name.

"He may want to cut any financial ties but with his appearance, he could never deny you as his father." Amelia heard a near chortle in her father's words. "Coming here, William, could not have been easy. I have misjudged you all these years and for that, I apologize. You have paid dearly for your indiscretion. I will consider what you are asking."

The bell clanged that would call Bidwell. With her cheeks damp with tears, she rushed away, hoping no one would impede her way to her bedchamber. She desperately needed time alone.

"Amelia, where are you going in such a rush?" her aunt asked, leaving the breakfast room as Amelia rushed by.

She slowed, lifting her gaze to her aunt.

"My dear, you have been crying. Tell me what is wrong."

"Please, come to my room with me," she whispered, not knowing if anyone else was nearby.

Libby took her niece's arm. Without a word, they climbed the stairs to Amelia's bed-chamber.

Once they were alone Amelia sank onto the edge of her bed. Her aunt sat next to her. After pulling a handkerchief from her sleeve and giving it to Amelia, she grasped her hand. "Talk to me."

Amelia wiped at her eyes and admitted her guilt at listening to the duke's and her father's conversation. Her aunt shook her head, her lips tightened in disapproval.

"As your elder, I must express my disapproval for listening in on a private conversation." She sighed. "As one woman to another, I might have done the same thing."

Amelia's eyes widened. She squeezed her hand and offered a grateful smile.

"I only knew part of the story, my dear," her aunt began. "I knew there was a competition between your father and Lord Radford. I also knew they both were infatuated with Georgetta. Her father was a tradesman and lived nearby. Being a few years older, I was often required to watch out for the younger ones when they played, especially near the water. Georgetta was such a pretty child and grew into a beautiful young woman. Your father and young William teased her mercilessly when they did not want her to follow them around, but they changed their tune as she matured. I am glad the two men have worked out their differences. Let us hope your father will agree to consider dropping the charges."

"I still have my questions, Aunt Libby. I did not get the impression from my time with Lucas that he was deceitful."

"So, you call him by his given name?"

Amelia bit into her lip before telling her the story of her sprained ankle. When she finished, she waited for the reprimand.

Instead, her aunt laughed.

"Aunt Libby!"

"My dear, I was young once. I cannot condone your actions. But a handsome man and a rebellious young lady both placed in such intimate situations, twice? First the stable incident and then this? I confess, your story would seem unbelievable if it were not true. It would be difficult to make up. Now, we must get on with our day. I believe your maid was searching for you earlier and from the looks of you, she needs to attend to your grooming. Oh, and one last bit of news. Your ring will be delivered this afternoon."

"Indeed, Aunt, that is another story."

****

The rest of the morning was busy with seeing to the guests' needs. After lunch, the ladies went to their rooms to rest before their grooming began for the ball. Amelia attended to the last-minute details and was ready to go to her bedchamber when Bidwell announced that her father wanted to see her in his study.

When she entered, both her father and brother were present and in conversation.

"Amelia, I have good news," her father said, smiling. "Lord Blakely's courier arrived a short time ago and the viscount has your mother's ring. He has asked for the honor of presenting it to you. Furthermore, he desires to court you and has asked for my permission."

"Father, no!"

"Allow me to finish. Since you have shown no inclination to find a husband, despite worthy offers, I am inclined to give him my blessing. He would not be my first choice, but you are not a spineless young woman. You could, perhaps, curb some of his excesses. His father, like me, is getting on in age."

"Please, Father, I find him annoying and egotistical to the extreme. I am grateful he is returning my ring, but I have no interest in his attentions."

Her father's tight-lipped expression and her brother's snicker demonstrated they had little interest in her opinion. She folded her arms firmly about her waist and breathed out a sigh of defiant resignation.

"Lord Blakely has requested the first dance this evening and told me he wants the pleasure of placing the ring on my finger. I have agreed to his two requests. I beg you, do not ask more of me."

Roderick gave a loud guffaw. "Leave it to the viscount. He never disappoints. I cannot disagree with your assessment of him, Amelia. He can grate on your sensibilities. He overindulges in food, drink, and rowdiness. He has gained a bit of a paunch since I last saw him too. Our brother-in-law, Drake, and Lord Hastings refuse to join in on another card game with him. They believe he cheats. His comments about winning the ring create suspicion that he may have used some trickery with his hand. Regardless, he is a bachelor, and if he is well-shackled, he can be tamed."

Amelia ignored his last comment before narrowing her eyes. "You do not believe he won the ring fairly?"

"Let me say his reputation for bluff and sly play follows him."

Her father raised a hand. "Roderick, enough about Blakely. Ellington does his best to direct his son on the right path. His mother has spoiled him. My friend agrees that you, Amelia, have the spunk to straighten the man out."

"I have no desire to be a reformer."

"You seem to have no desire to marry anyone. You can no longer use the excuse of your mother's passing to avoid suitors. If you wait much longer, you will be considered on the shelf. Younger debutantes will be chosen before you."

"I should return to our guests." The thought of Lord Blakely's courtship was enough to make her ill.

"I called you in here, for another reason," the earl said, forcing her to stop in her escape and turn around. "Roderick is already aware of my news. As you may have heard, the Duke of Radford came to see me early this morning. He asked me to drop the charges against his son. Roderick delivered my message to the constable about noon. Mr. Grey will be released today."

Amelia's heart lurched before she exhaled a calming breath. She dearly hoped she'd hid her relief well. "I…I do not know what to say. Since the ring has been returned, I suppose the matter has been dealt with."

"Radford will deal with his son." Her father, who had been standing by the fireplace with her brother, returned to his desk. "I have some final business to take care of before preparing for the gala. I am quite proud of your preparations for this evening, Amelia. You have honored both me and your mother, God rest her soul."

Amelia gave a grateful nod, though her father's suggestion about Blakely as a suitor grated on her nerves.

She left the room, a plan brewing in her mind.

Chapter 16

Sneering, Constable Withers unlocked Lucas's jail cell. "The Earl of Weatherly has dropped the charges against you. You are free to go."

Lucas remained in place, his brows curved, while he took in the words.

"You have nothing to say? I was preparing to transport you to a hulk where you'd be placed in irons."

Lucas shrugged and left the cell. "I hope you don't expect me to thank you."

Withers grunted. "Save your gratitude for your deliverer. The fee for your keep has been paid. Few of my prisoners are transported home in such style."

Confused, but not wasting another word on Withers, Lucas brushed the fetid straw from his trousers and strode toward the door, giving only a passing glance to Wither's deputy before leaving the building. He raised an arm to cover his eyes. The sun's bright glare, after living in the dark for over a week, blinded him. Adjusting his gaze, he spotted the black carriage with the ducal emblem emblazoned on its door. A coachman dressed in fine livery stood waiting, with the carriage door ajar.

"What the hell?" Lucas came close to marching back inside until his mother's face appeared through the carriage window. He hesitated, his fists gripped to his sides, the taste of bile in his throat. He swallowed down his disgust and climbed into the carriage ready to spit out his rage.

His mother read his expression immediately and raised a hand. "Lucas, control your anger. Sit, and let me explain."

His head jerked when the carriage door snapped shut. He plunked down on the red velvet cushioned seat and faced his mother. "Explain? You allowed him to pay my way out? How could you? Will there never be an end to what I owe that man?"

"It is not what you think."

"His noble stature was enough?"

He seethed as the carriage surged forward and they bounced in their seats. *Indeed, the power of nobility has no limits*. He took in the elegance of the plush carriage interior. How humiliated his father must have been to hear that his illegitimate mistake had been labeled a thief.

"Did you go to him or did the rumors reach him?"

His mother exhaled. "I was prepared to go to Lady Pierce's father and beg him to drop the charges. I may never have told you. Lord Weatherly, your father, and I grew up together. Lord Weatherly was just Charles to me then. I thought it best to speak with your father first. The news had not reached him yet." She looked away.

Lucas recognized anguish behind her words. Appealing to his father for assistance could not have been easy for her.

"I told him you were innocent," she said, refocusing on her son. "He went to see the earl. Lord Weatherly agreed to drop the charges and let your father deal with the situation."

"You mean, deal with me. He plans to be my

disciplinarian?" Lucas snickered.

"My son, you are free from that horrid place. We are going home. You need to strip out of those grime-ridden clothes, take a bath, and get some rest. Then we will discuss the matter further."

"Discuss his interference? I appreciate your devotion to me, Mother, but I could have worked it out and bore anything to avoid his aid. Is he not satisfied I have lost my position at the stables, or does he plan to fix that too? At what price, and why are we riding in the ducal carriage? What does he want from you?"

"Iris is making you a hearty meal," Georgetta said, with narrowed eyes, pressed lips, and crossed arms.

Since childhood, when he wanted his way, she gave him that look, ending the conversation. He wanted to say more. He needed an explanation. His mother's careworn appearance silenced him, and he was responsible. He had directed his anger toward her rather than where it belonged. He had no desire to face his sire, but it must be done, and he would not be restrained.

They sat in uneasy silence for the rest of the journey home. With frayed nerves wound tighter than the springs under his father's well-sprung carriage, he drummed his fingers on his knee until his mother reached out a hand to stop his agitation. Lucas crossed his arms and smirked. He sat on his father's red velvet seat in trousers likely infested with vermin from the filthy cell. Better if Tom from the stables had come to retrieve him. Then he realized he would have had no right to ask. He no longer worked there.

When they reached the cottage, the carriage driver opened the door and helped his mother out. Lucas gave a dismissive nod to the man before taking his mother's arm. Without a word, the servant mounted the carriage and drove away.

After bathing for an hour, scrubbing the past days from his body, he changed into clean clothes and joined his mother at their dining table. Iris welcomed him home and set a place for him. He offered a grateful smile and gazed at his mother. Dark circles under her eyes proved she had slept little while he was imprisoned. He swore inwardly at the worry he had caused her.

Nearing fifty, she was still attractive. Silver strands mingled with her dark brown hair pulled back in a bun. The fine lines around her mouth appeared deeper today.

His thoughts drifted to what his father's wife must have enjoyed. While his mother wore simple dresses of practical fabric, *she* would have worn silks and lace. Jewels had most likely dripped from the duchess's earlobes and neckline, while her mother wore only a small gold pendant around her neck.

He stared at the pendant. He had never thought to ask her about it, most likely because she had worn it always. To him, it was as much a part of her as her fair skin. A family heirloom, perhaps, from a grandmother.

He had hoped to buy his mother fine clothing and jewels. He had believed if Winston was true to his word, he would soon run the stables.

He even imagined becoming a member of the gentry if his dreams of expanding the business had come to be. Now, he would be lucky to find a job shoveling manure. He pushed his dish aside, and his mother looked up.

"Thank the Lord; you are home and safe, Lucas.

You must rest. I doubt you slept in that horrible place."

"And did you sleep while I was away, Mother?"

"We will both sleep tonight. Tomorrow we shall talk."

Chapter 17

As the musicians prepared to begin, Amelia breathed a sigh of relief. All had gone well. New arrivals had been introduced, and the guests conversed in the grand drawing room.

"How lovely you look, my dear," Aunt Libby said, coming to her side. "Your gown was fitted to perfection, considering we had little time for alterations."

Amelia smiled, "I may have fought being sent off to London, but I am grateful to you and your *modiste*." She gave her aunt an admiring glance. I love the amethyst beading on your lavender silk. So elegant. I should have invited your Dr. Curtis. Too much was on my mind."

"He is not my Dr. Curtis," Libby said, with a faint blush. "Ah, the musicians have begun to play, and Lord Blakely is heading this way."

Amelia rolled her eyes before forcing a welcoming smile. She noticed the buttons on his evening coat looked as if they were about to pop.

"Lady Amelia, you look enchanting." He bowed. "May I take your hand?"

He led her to the dance floor. Amelia made certain the first dance was a quadrille, where other couples were involved, and she could stay a good distance apart from the viscount for most of the set.

"I must ask the musicians to play a waltz," he said when the first set was completed. "I hope you will honor me with that dance as well."

"We shall see." She doubted her feet could take more of his maneuvering after his clumsy steps in the quadrille. "Might we take a stroll? I believe you have something for me," she said in a low, purposely seductive voice.

She smelled alcohol on his breath as he drew closer, before leading her off the dance floor and to the open doors of the drawing room. She was pleased. She wanted him to have a loose tongue.

"Let us find a more secluded spot where we can talk privately. Perhaps, the library?"

"I must remain in clear view of the ballroom for appearance's sake. I am sure you understand." She demurely tilted her head and pointed to a settee in an alcove in full view of the drawing room entrance.

Blakely frowned but nodded and led her to the settee.

"I am so grateful my ring ended up in your hands." She smiled and edged closer to the arm of the seat.

"Yes, fortunately, in my hands." His gaze dipped to her décolletage. "You look ravishing, my dear."

Her bodice revealed more than she wished in a sitting position. She fingered her pearl earring, momentarily blocking his view of her bodice. "To think my treasured heirloom should be in the hands of a scoundrel who thought nothing more of it than to gamble it away. You must tell me about your poker hand. I want to hear all the details of how you won my ring."

He beamed at her request, adjusted his seat, and his

knee brushed against hers. She wanted to flinch. Instead, she remained still. His smile that dangled on the corner of his lips made her want to retch. She must give a semblance of an attraction despite her distaste.

"Please, Lord Blakely, I beg you. Do not keep me waiting."

His eyes widened.

"Your poker hand, sir. I am curious as to how you were able to win my ring back for me. You must be a skilled poker player. I know little of the game."

She hoped her feigned interest might draw out his boastful nature, but he appeared to have only one thing on his mind.

"I would be most pleased if you would call me Frederick."

She curved her lips into a coquettish simper. "Frederick, you must be a top card player."

"Skilled, my lovely, in the tricks of the game," he said smugly. "Truthfully, it was quite an enjoyable steal if you care to know. Indeed, too easy. The fool I won it from was bacon-brained and more in his cups than I. He was convinced he would win the entire pot when he tossed the ring on the table. He wore the look of a conqueror." Blakely spouted a snuffling guffaw. "I had to bring him down to size."

"But why did he not add more coins rather than a piece of jewelry? Is this common?" She was acting bacon-brained herself, but she had succeeded in drawing out his arrogance and pride.

"He was out of blunt. I knew him only by reputation. He is a common sort who uses his good looks and affable personality to wheedle into polite society. His only claim to sordid fame is his kinship to the Duke of Radford's by-blow. I cannot recall his name, but he pulled out the ring and bragged how he had lifted it from his half-brother's pocket. I had to refrain from revealing my glee." He drew his head back and snorted.

Amelia noticed the button on his evening coat hung on by a thread.

"The fool boasted about spreading his winnings into the Duke of Radford's bastard's face." Blakely folded his hands together and flayed his fingers out as if he were spreading a hand of cards. "One thief stole from another thief, and with my skillful trickery, I stole it from both of them."

She had heard enough. "I appreciate your willingness to return my cherished ring. My father would gladly compensate you." She removed her glove and held out her splayed fingers.

Wearing a confident grin, he pulled it from his coat pocket. Taking her hand in his, he lowered it to just below his belly. If he had been slimmer, her hand would have rested on his crotch. He placed the ring on her finger but did not let go.

She snatched her hand away. "Thank you, Frederick. Now, I must return to the ball." She began to rise.

He grasped her arm too firmly and drew closer, his boozy breath blowing in her face. "Not so soon, my sweet." He gazed at the open door of the drawing room. "Might we share a kiss instead of mere words of gratitude?"

She stared at his hand that held her arm. "That would be most inappropriate."

"I understand you have been trained in modesty,

but your attentiveness has demonstrated your desire. Let us find a more isolated place."

She gritted her teeth. "I shall be forced to scream if you do not release my arm."

He abruptly dropped his hold. "Forgive me if I offended."

She ignored his stony expression and made no reply before scurrying back into the ballroom. As she breathed out a heavy exhale, her sister Eva rushed over to her.

"Amelia, I was looking for you. Where have you been?" She took a closer look at her sister's face. "You look pale. What is wrong?"

Amelia gathered her wits and smiled. "Nothing, nothing at all. I simply needed to outfox a fool."

****

The ball was a success and the late dinner received with much praise. After the invited gentry left for home, and the houseguests retired, Amelia crawled into bed near three in the morning. She fell asleep immediately from exhaustion, only to wake two hours later. Her ring's return should be the end of the debacle, but she was in turmoil. No, angry. Angry at Lucas Grey. Why did he take the ring to London instead of returning it to her? He said nothing of it when he brought her home after her jumping accident.

After fisting her pillow, she plopped her head down and closed her eyes, then tossed, turned, and threw her covers over her head, to no avail. She sat up. The house would remain quiet until at least noon. The servants were given the morning to sleep since they were up all night. With a houseful of guests, she would have no other time to escape without a dozen questions, and without a chaperone.

Though excruciating, her meeting with Blakely resulted in additional news that created more questions. From what the viscount said, Grey's stepbrother stole the ring from him. Had Lucas planned to sell it while he was in London? He claims his innocence, but why would he take it with him and say nothing to her when he saw her last. It must have been to sell it.

He was out of jail, and she was determined to confront him. He'd led her to believe he was honorable and caring. She was foolish enough to waste hours and days brooding and thinking of him endlessly. Early morning might be the only time she could sneak out for a few hours without being noticed.

Amelia rose, washed, and dressed quickly. After listening for any sign of movement, she slipped out through the servants' quarters. It was a cold day and still dark but, thankfully, not frigid. The dawn mist was lifting by the time she saddled Cinnamon. After stepping up and gripping the sides of the stall, she mounted with little problem. Having left the stable doors open, she rode off slowly until she was clear of the house. She had about three hours, and she would not waste a minute.

Lucas's home was closer than Winston's stables, at most, a half-hour ride. The cold air was invigorating and dispelled any tiredness she felt from little sleep. A route through fields would shorten the ride. The only obstacle was a narrow stream she was forced to cross, which muddied her riding skirt and boots.

When the cottage came in sight, her apprehension grew. By the time she reached the low rock wall that bordered the small cottage, her heart was in her throat.

The idiocy of her actions hit her harder than the wind that had picked up during her ride. For one thing, he did not live alone. And what would she say to Mrs. Montrose, Lucas's mother? What would the woman think of her appearing at her door before seven in the morning? This was lunacy. Grey had only been released yesterday. His mother must have been heartsick that her son was imprisoned.

She had become so worked up by Lord Blakely's admission and had spent too many days and nights with conflicting thoughts. She was behaving irrationally and without thinking it through. Just what her father accused her of too often. It was scandalous for her to visit Lucas's home, not to mention ill-mannered to intrude. How often had she been scolded by both parents for her impulsiveness? At twenty, she should know better. She allowed emotions to lead and common sense to follow, often too late. With all the busy-ness, the guests, the gala, the questions, no sleep, she had not been thinking at all. Her heart was ruling her head.

But it was not too late.

She could be home and back in her bed before anyone stirred. Amelia pulled at the reins and turned Cinnamon about, to start a slower journey back. The cold air had brought her to her senses.

"Lady Pierce. Leaving so soon?"

She jerked her head back to see Lucas standing on the front step of the cottage in a nightshirt that hung over his trousers.

Oh no! She glanced at the road and back at Lucas, who stood with his hands on his hips staring at her. Swallowing hard, she led her horse the short distance up the stone drive.

Lucas met her and reached for the horse's reins. "I observed you from my window. You appeared to be making a hard decision." He patted Cinnamon's mane. "I could only half-dress to stop you from riding off. Will you grant me a few minutes to finish dressing? I am more than curious to know why you have graced my doorstep this morning. "

Amelia shivered and it wasn't from the wind or the cold but from the fear of facing him. She bit into her bottom lip and nodded and he led the horse to a post to tie. When he reached up to help her down, she shook her head. She would wait for him, but she wanted the ability to ride off as swiftly as needed. He stared at her for a long moment, the muscles in his face tightening. Saying nothing more, he returned to the house.

To face him and find out the truth had possessed her and led her to make a fool of herself. She stared at the tied reins and wished she'd ridden off. After seeing his drawn face, her anger, and whatever imaginings she had created of deception, were lost to the reality of his situation. He appeared weary, his confident vigor gone. What must it have been like for him in jail?

In their previous encounters, she had imagined there was something powerful between them. She'd never felt such desire in the presence of any of the suitors that had called on her after her coming out. Perhaps she was drawn to a sense of danger over decorum, or recklessness over civility? Her brother often accused her of as much. Like shrill voices or a discordant cacophony of sounds, her mind pulled her in different directions until the door opened, and Lucas stepped out fully dressed. A large dog scooted out from behind him.

"That's Molly," Lucas said, as the Golden Retriever ran toward Cinnamon, barking and backing up when the horse snorted. "Molly, go. Do your business!"

The dog obeyed and ran off through the yard. Lucas gazed at her muddy skirt and boots before approaching her. With ease, he unhooked her right leg, withdrew her left foot from of the stirrup, and held out his arms. She paused before gripping his shoulders and allowing him to lift her to the ground. He did not immediately let go of her, Instead, he gazed into her eyes, deeply, as if he were trying to read her thoughts.

"Come in. I have stoked the fire in the parlor so you can warm up. Iris, our housekeeper, will clean up those muddy boots."

"It would not be appropriate for me to enter your house," she said, embarrassed and dumbstruck at his offer.

"Iris is in the kitchen, preparing a tray of coffee and biscuits. You are safe. My mother is dressing. She will be down soon."

"Oh, dear. What she must think of me, interrupting your household so early, and so soon after your release. I must apologize to her."

"And not me?" He raised his brow. "No need to reply. My mother does not make judgments. We are both wondering what your visit is all about."

"I…"

"You can explain inside." He took her arm and led her to the door.

As she entered the front hall, Molly followed close behind, wagging her tail. Amelia stooped to pet her and was greeted with sloppy kisses and squeals of excitement.

Lucas grabbed her collar. "She's a friendly sort. Molly, leave our guest alone. Sit." Again, the dog obeyed,

"She is quite obedient," Amelia said, grateful the dog helped to relieve some of the tension she felt upon entering. She glimpsed to her left and viewed a comfortable room with ivory-painted walls, and tufted furnishings and flames roaring in the fireplace. A short, plump, black-haired woman wearing an apron, scurried into the hall from a door on the right.

"Don't mind Molly, milady. She is part of the family. Let me take your coat and hat. If you take a seat by the fire, I shall remove those wet boots. Once you are settled, I'll bring some coffee to warm you up. Unless you prefer a cup of tea?"

Amelia could barely think. "Coffee is fine. Please do not go to any trouble."

"No trouble at all. The house is just waking up. We all need to break our fast. Here is the lady of the house now."

A slim woman of medium height, wearing a simple brown day dress, descended the hall stairs.

"My mother, Georgetta Montrose," Lucas said, as his mother stopped before her. With brows knitted, she gave a slight curtsy.

"Please, Mrs. Montrose, I do not deserve a curtsy for interrupting your household. I should have waited for a more appropriate time. I must apologize. I had some questions I hoped to ask your son. I realize, it was wrong of me to come, especially at this time."

To Amelia's surprise, the woman gave her an understanding smile. "I believe we all have questions.

Waiting for answers only creates more. Allow Iris to take your coat. And Lucas, show your guest to a seat by the fire."

"I should keep my coat. I cannot stay long."

"Have you once again escaped the estate in secret?" Lucas jeered. "Lady Amelia Pierce is not fond of the narrow restrictions expected for the daughter of an earl."

"Your coat will be only steps away, dear," his mother said, ignoring her son's jibe.

After Iris took her coat, Lucas led her to a seat by the fire. He bent and removed her boots. It reminded her of the time he knelt to check her ankle injury. But unlike his energetic visage at the training ring, his shoulders were hunched as if in defeat. She brought to mind that he had lost his position at Winston Stables. He placed her boots on the hearth and took a seat opposite hers. His mother, who had been standing nearby, excused herself to help Iris in the kitchen. Amelia suspected she wanted to give them a few minutes alone.

She felt suddenly like the guilty party but she had no reason, except for intruding on their privacy. His presence so near her was disconcerting.

"I understand you lost your position at the stables, Mr. Grey, an unfortunate outcome."

"When you were saddled on my horse, a breath away from me, I thought we agreed you would you call me Lucas."

She lowered her head and smoothed the folds of her skirt, remembering well. "You became a friend who helped me then. Are you still a friend? Please explain how my ring ended up in your possession and in

London to be gambled away."

"Ah, these are the burning questions that brought you here. Does it matter now? Indeed, your father must be quite satisfied I am labeled a thief and have lost my income."

His utterance was harsh but with an edge of despondency, he could not mask. She gazed down at her clutched hands and spotted the nub of her ring beneath her glove. How odd that this morning she had forgotten the jeweled ring was back on her finger, while the viscount's words and actions were set like a stone in her mind.

"You have not answered my questions."

"I did not mean to draw on your sympathy as your face reveals, or sound like a victim instead of the villain that I am."

How could he read her so well? "Are you a villain?" she asked. "From what I have heard, you claim your innocent of theft, but without explanation."

He leaned back in his seat and rubbed his unshaven chin as if he were contemplating his response. "I found your ring after your brother pulled you from my arms and carried you off. I planned to return it. After experiencing your brother's fury and condescending glare, I decided to wait a few days until tempers cooled. John Winston was unwell at the time. He sent me off to London the next day to meet his scheduled appointments. Your ring was in my possession and would have been returned when I got back. Why I did not leave it at home, I cannot explain. Perhaps, I enjoyed the warmth of it in my inside pocket next to my heart, until I could see you again, and place it on your finger." He gave her a slanted grin. "Does that answer your question?"

She fingered the embroidery on her cuff and wished the warmth rising in her cheeks could be blamed on the heat of the fire. "You met with your stepbrother there."

"He offered me a place to stay for a few days while I completed my business."

Lucas paused when Iris appeared. She placed a tray on the table between them and poured two cups of coffee.

"These biscuits just came out of the oven. Please enjoy before they grow cold," she urged, before going to the hearth and reaching for Amelia's boots. "I shall have these cleaned up for you before you leave."

"Thank you." She smiled at the warm-hearted housekeeper.

"How awful it must have been for you to be locked up," she said once Iris had left the room. "Your father—"

"So, you heard of my father's interference," he snapped. "His pride could not stomach the shame I was bringing to his name."

"No, that is untrue!" Amelia covered her mouth.

Lucas leaned forward. "What do you know of it? What did the duke offer your father to bring my release?"

"As is my constant fault, I speak before I think."

"I plan to confront the duke. I shall find out his method of bribery. And if I can find a way to repay it, I will."

The fury in his voice and his hard expression at the mention of his sire startled her.

"Your coffee is getting cold," Lucas rested back in

his chair, his lips curled as if he realized he had lost a modicum of control. He sipped his coffee and ate a biscuit before reaching for another. "Excuse me for my indulgence, but the food at the jail was far from appealing."

Amelia bit into her bottom lip, wondering if he had eaten at all while he was incarcerated. She took a sip of her lukewarm coffee.

"You have more on your mind. Do not keep me in suspense."

She set down her cup. "Your brother, your stepbrother, I mean. You did not give him the ring to sell, did you?"

Lucas stopped chewing and dropped the remaining biscuit on his plate. "Where did you hear this?"

"From the viscount who won it and gave it back to me. He said your stepbrother admitted stealing it from you before he gambled it away."

A muffled gasp caused them to turn toward the sound. Georgetta stood in the doorway.

"Lucas, is this the part of the story you refused to reveal?" His mother, frowning, walked into the room. "I suspected as much. It appears Lady Pierce has put into words what I have been waiting patiently to hear from your lips."

"Mother, this is my business."

"Your business? You accept the loss of all you have gained to protect Graham?"

"He protected me in years past. I have paid him in full."

His mother shook her head, despair written on her face. "I have more to say, later." She left the room.

Amelia cringed. What had she caused? He had

personal reasons for giving up his freedom for another. These were family matters. Not her business. She stood, dropping the napkin she had placed on her lap.

"Forgive me. I have caused friction in your home." She turned toward the door before gazing down at her stockinged feet. "Please, ask your housekeeper to bring my things."

Lucas rose as quickly. He strode to her side, turning her gently to him. He wiped a tear from her cheek. "My beautiful minx. How your father must have aged trying to keep you under his protection and out of trouble."

He drew her close to him. She went willingly when he wrapped her in his arms and kissed her in a way she could only imagine in her wildest dreams. Then he loosened his hold.

"Now, I have reason to apologize."

She looked up at his hooded eyes and the errant wave of black hair that fell over his forehead. A small voice she ignored too often told her to pull away, to be stunned at his offense. Instead, she gazed at his lips, wanting more. He dropped his arms and stepped back.

"I'll go find your things."

When he left her standing there, she remembered to breathe.

Once outside, he helped her onto her saddle. She refused his request to drive her home in a buggy or to fetch his horse to see her safely home. She needed time alone, to think.

"I ask you, Lady Amelia Pierce, to keep your suspicions and what you heard to yourself." He handed her the reins.

She nodded, remaining silent, and led Cinnamon to

the road. There was nothing more she could say. She accepted his explanation and believed him. He had planned to return the ring. She'd gotten her answers while creating chaos in his home. All took second place to his kiss.

My beautiful minx. His words, his eyes, his arms holding her, wrapped her in warmth as she rode home. Her father was wrong. She was not opposed to being courted or marrying, just not by men for whom she felt nothing. Lucas Grey was different. Her father would never understand.

When she arrived home, she cared little if she was found out. Once Cinnamon was taken care of, she re-entered the house and returned to her room, still unnoticed. It was not yet ten in the morning. The house remained quiet. She suspected Cook might be in the kitchen preparing food for the breakfast room. As she removed her riding outfit, lingering thoughts of Lucas's kiss and the warmth she saw in his eyes remained.

She returned to her bed and wrapped the coverlet around her, but doubted she could sleep. She needed a plan. Lucas was innocent, not a thief freed as a favor to his father. The answers she had sought only brought a greater challenge. She'd promised Lucas not to reveal the truth. She could not break that promise. There had to be another way. He'd lost his livelihood over her carelessness.

What could she do to repair the damage?

Chapter 18

Amelia sat in the library appreciating an hour of quiet. She closed the book she was reading and smoothed a hand over the cover of Wollstonecraft's book, *On the Vindication of the Rights of Women*.

Did this author really believe men could change? She scowled as she considered her experiences with the men in her family and, presently, the viscount's offensive behavior.

Snow threatened, and she feared the final guests would forego their plans to leave in the morning. Except Lady Lenora Hastings, most of the female guests had left the day before. Eva and her husband had taken Aunt Libby to visit a friend who lived nearby. She would be gone until tomorrow, returning only for a day to pack and return to London.

The men who remained, Hastings, Ellington, and his son, Blakely, were on an outing with her father, leaving Lady Hastings for Amelia to entertain. Thankfully, the woman was in her bedchamber packing.

Unable to concentrate on her reading, she tried to turn her thoughts on tasks that needed to be completed before Christmas Day, especially personal gifts for her family and the household servants. Instead, her thoughts returned to Lucas Grey's misfortune. She set the book aside, walked to one of the high, tapestry-draped windows, and gazed at the gray sky and leafless trees.

"November must be the dreariest month of the year," she murmured, wrapping her arms around herself. The holiday season revelry did little to negate her melancholy.

Knowing Grey had lost his livelihood and was labeled a thief, simply for helping her, was agonizing. He would not be in such dire straits if he hadn't stopped to help her that afternoon when she was crawling around in the hay. If she hadn't allowed her anger to control her actions, her ring would have most likely stayed on her finger. Perhaps, they would still be strangers, only nodding to each other at Winston's when she accompanied her brother to an event. Her father's demand that he be arrested would never have occurred.

Still, she could not regret coming to know him. He'd unlocked feelings she could not ignore. She had no reason to even see him again. She sighed as a leaf, blown by the wind, fell to the ground. His kiss had been unexpected and so memorable. It had been her first. True, he had a rakish reputation with women. To him, it most likely meant nothing. Even if he returned her feelings, they could never be together. Her father would forbid his suit. Amelia gasped when a hand rested on her shoulder. She spun around, brushing against the viscount's lapels. "Lord Blakely!"

"I apologize for startling you. How pleasant to find you alone."

"Your closeness is inappropriate," she snapped, raising her ringed hand to urge distance.

He gripped it, smoothing his thumb over the rim of

the emerald ring. "I remember, Lady Amelia, slipping this ring on your finger ever so slowly, and the coquettish look you gave me as we sat so close together. Do you remember, my dear?"

As she jerked her hand away, the library door creaked. She tried to step around him, but he drew her roughly to his chest and wrapped his arms around her. Her attempt to scream was silenced when he covered her mouth with his.

"Oh, heavens!"

Blakely released his lips, but not his hold.

Amelia wrenched herself from him. Lenora Hastings glared at her, wide-eyed and mouth gaping. Blakely's arms dropped.

"Lady Hastings!" he barked, rushing towards the woman. "I plead for your discretion. I assure you of my honor…"

Before Amelia could catch her breath or utter a word, he grasped the woman's arm and hauled her toward the open library door, his words dissolving as the door slammed behind them.

Alone, and frozen in place, Amelia stared at the door, her arms clutched to her breast. A sob tore from her lips as she relived the assault and envisioned the horror on Lenora's face. She stumbled to a nearby chair, gripped it and clung to its back. She could still feel his suffocating grip, his slobbering mouth on hers. Her body shivered and her stomach roiled.

Had Lenora seen her distress and that he had forced himself on her? Was she already imagining how the woman would deliver her first-hand account? She had to think… had to find her father. Why was Blakely here? He was to have gone hunting with the men. And

Lady Hastings, the worst of all gossipers, witnessed his blatant attack. Blakely's mass had blocked any appearance of her attempt to push him away. It may have looked as if she welcomed his embrace. Lenora would delight in telling others what she witnessed. Her father and brother would demand the viscount marry her to save her from ruin.

Another thought terrified her when she remembered his words. Was she responsible? She had played a flirtatious game at the ball so he would reveal information. Although she had ignored his casual advances since. he hadn't forgotten. He'd be duty-bound to marry her. Fear and loathing clutched at her insides. She needed air. Amelia fled from the room to the entry hall, and pulled open the front door, when the housekeeper appeared.

"Milady? Where are you going? You're crying. What is wrong?"

"I must find my father." With quivering fingers, she gripped the door handle.

"Not without a coat and hat, milady. A footman will find him for you."

"No!" She rushed out the door.

She had to get away from the house. Away from that horrible man.

"Your coat!" the housekeeper called.

Amelia ignored her. She ran down the drive, nearly tripping on the stones. Righting herself, she kept running. Tears blinded her. A sudden shout and a clamber of hooves broke into her hysteria.

She zigzagged to avoid them and leaped back when the carriage door flung open, nearly slamming into her. A strong arm grabbed hers.

"Let me go!" she screamed.

"You are in no condition to be running off, Lady Pierce. What is wrong?"

"I…" Amelia sucked in a breath, and gaped at Lord Radford, unable to speak. She had no idea what she was doing, only that she needed to escape.

"You are about to collapse. Come," he said kindly, leading her to the carriage door. "Let me bring you back to the house."

"No! He is still in there," she sobbed.

"He?" Radford's brow furrowed. "Allow my coachman to take us on a short ride." He nodded up at the driver. Taking her arm, he urged her into the carriage.

The duke shut the door. He pulled off his coat and wrapped it over her shoulders. She shivered more from fear than cold.

Sitting across from her, he handed her his handkerchief. "Catch your breath and tell me what happened."

She sniffed into the handkerchief, unable to meet his gaze.

"I want to help you, my dear."

She saw compassion in his expression. She wiped her eyes, took a deep inward breath, and exhaled. "He assaulted me. I think he might have planned it so I would be compromised, and we would have to marry. He is the most horrible man. I fear my father will demand it," she blurted out. She brushed strands of hair away from her face. The realization that she was in the duke's carriage telling him, of all people, what happened, struck her suddenly. "Forgive me. I just don't know what to do."

"You should not be sorry for anything. Your father is a reasonable man. You must tell him what occurred. I am a witness to the result of the brute's behavior, am I not? I can testify you were not a willing party."

Amelia sat stunned at his caring demeanor. He believed her. She recalled how she had spied on him during his visit to see her father. "You will talk to Father?" she whispered.

He nodded, taking her hand in his.

Amelia tried to absorb the duke's words. Could he truly help her? She didn't even know him, having never spoken to him before, only listened rudely to a private conversation. And now she was ready to beg him for his help.

"Who is this man?"

"Frederick Blakely, Lord Ellington's son." Rage, for a moment, overtook the crippling fear. "Lady Hastings walked in and saw him, crushed against me…" She shuddered, remembering. "I could be forced to marry him." She dropped her head into her hands, shame and repulsion eating at her insides.

"Blakely, you say. The viscount. He is the reason for my visit. I have questions for him."

Amelia wiped her eyes and nose with his handkerchief. "Is it to help Lucas?"

"Yes. I do not hear animosity toward my son in your question."

"Indeed, no, Your Grace. He is innocent and should never have been put in jail."

Radford smiled. "You call him by his first name? You are friends?"

She bit into her bottom lip. "I mean, Mr. Grey. I have come to know his character. He is a good man."

"Hmm, I see. Despite the tears that have made your cheeks nearly raw in the cold, I hear a tenderness in your words. You have strong feelings for him."

She sniffed. She had lost complete control of her actions and her words, but nothing mattered now. She was facing the horror of marrying the viscount. "Yes, I do, but my father would never understand."

"Let me deal with your father. I think it is time we return to the estate."

"Father is not home. I fear going back there."

"I shall be by your side. Perhaps we can have tea in your father's study while we wait for him. On second thought, you might want to retire to your bedchamber. You have been through quite an ordeal. I shall take care of the viscount, and I know Lord Hastings well." He gave a calculating grin. "I promise he will want to put a stop to any of his wife's gossip."

Amelia wondered if he knew something improper about Lord Hastings.

"Shall we return?"

She sighed and nodded.

"Do not fear. We shall work this out."

****

As they entered the house, Amelia braced herself for what was to come. Bidwell appeared immediately. His narrowed eyes told her she must look disheveled, her face raw from her tears. Bidwell's posture straightened as he greeted the duke.

"Your Grace, your visit is unexpected. My lord should be returning soon, however, if you care to wait."

"I have not come to see Weatherly but to see Viscount Blakely. I understand he is here."

"I shall notify him immediately. May I take your

coat?"

"Not necessary. I prefer we meet in Weatherly's study, for privacy." The duke turned to Amelia, a look of kind dismissal in his nod.

She understood. Ignoring Bidwell's questioning look, she stepped away from the duke. As she scurried to her room, she wished she had told Bidwell not to call on her maid. He might well do so after seeing her appearance.

Once in her room, she poured water into her basin and scrubbed her face, not only to wash away her tears but the remembrance of Blakely's mouth on hers. After grabbing her towel, she sat on the edge of her bed and pressed it against her lips and squinting eyes. Tossing the woven linen aside, she gazed at the ceiling and inhaled deep. How was the duke to deal with Blakely? And Lady Hastings may have already spread the news to whoever would listen in the household. She may have even written a post to friends. Enough. She could not sit here and wonder what was happening below. After a brief look in her mirror to pin stray curls back from her face, she left the room only to nearly walk into her maid.

"Bidwell summoned me, milady. He said you were visibly upset. You look harried and pale. Perhaps a warm bath would be advisable?"

"I am fine. Edith. Please, go about your day."

Without another word, she descended the staircase and walked silently to her father's study. She knew she was behaving badly, but it was her life at stake. She would not be kept in the dark. Grasping the handle of the door, Amelia paused. Instead of pushing it open as her reactive mind wanted her to do, she eased it open an inch, enough to hear voices within.

"Your Grace, I was surprised and honored by your request to see me."

Amelia drew in a silent sigh. Blakely must have just entered the room. She was grateful for Edith's interference. She might have come face to face with him.

She drew her ear to the door and listened.

"I came to discuss one matter with you, Blakely," the duke said with authority. "But we must dispense with another first."

Amelia shrank back at the sound of a scuffle and a choking sound erupted from within. She leaned in again and easing the door open, she peered in. The duke had his hands at Blakely's neckcloth, twisting it until redness rose from the man's neck to his chin.

"I understand you treated a lady, very unladylike," the duke said in a gruff tone.

Blakely's eyes bulged before the duke loosened his hold and pushed the shorter man into the chair behind him.

"You must allow me to defend myself." Blakely sniveled, straightening his neckcloth.

Radford stood over him. "I expect you to apologize to Lady Pierce in the presence of her father and Lady Hastings. Once you do so and our business concludes, I suggest you pack your bags and leave the premises. I suspect the earl will agree when he hears about your disgraceful behavior."

Blakely adjusted his seat and cleared his throat. "Your Grace, may I say that I hold myself above such tasteless behavior as occurred with Lady Amelia. I assumed, however…"

The duke put a finger to his lips. "I assume you want your courtesy title to remain unblemished. If I hear you spout off any offensive falsehoods about the earl's daughter, I shall personally make certain you are shamed throughout the royal kingdom. Do I make myself clear?"

Blakely's lips compressed, his face reddening as if he were holding back a barrage of justifications before his shoulders slumped. He nodded.

"Good. The matter is settled." Radford walked to the hearth, a few feet away, and rested an arm on the mantle.

She drew the door close, just wide enough to listen, her heart in her throat.

"Now to the other matter," the duke said.

Amelia knew she should leave. She pinched her lips together and stayed by the door, too curious to walk away. She never thought eavesdropping was one of her vices, but it was becoming a habit.

"I want an accounting of the events that led you to acquire the lost ring. Tell me all that occurred during your game of cards."

Blakely cleared his throat. She imagined him straightening his neckcloth and sitting straighter in the seat he'd been pushed into. She suppressed a satisfied smirk.

"I must begin by saying, I could never have imagined joining in on a poker game would have involved me in such a sordid affair. I was appalled to discover the emerald ring I won belonged to the Earl of Weatherly's daughter, a woman I most admire despite my ill-advised behavior today."

Amelia swallowed down a retching knot in her

throat at the fool's mendacious blathering.

"Go on," the duke said stonily.

"I offered to return it without compensation. Please know that Lady Amanda granted me the honor of placing it on her finger."

Amelia pressed her lips together, her insides steaming at his suggestive tone.

"The details, Blakely. Tell me about the man who tossed the ring in the pot. Everything you can remember."

After describing the situation and repeating Lucas's stepbrother's boasts, the viscount guffawed as if he was enjoying his remembrances. "I have found if I appear more soused than my opponents, they believe they can take advantage. The man was a dupe. The chump's expression changed from an over-confident smirk to slobbering desperation when he saw I held a better hand. He begged for another game, hoping he could win the ring back. He had nothing to bet. I left the establishment, quite sober."

"The man admitted he had acquired the ring from his stepbrother? Explain." From the duke's tone, he was ignoring the viscount's ego-inflated comments, while Amelia rolled her eyes at Blakely's arrogance.

"He professed he had filched it from him. He bragged that his brother would be forgiving when he presented his winnings. I admit I can understand his reasoning."

"What do you mean?" The duke's raised voice carried a simmering fury.

Amelia pressed her hands to her lips to smother a gasp.

"Lord Radford, why would the ring be in London

in the first place if the bastard had not expected to sell it?"

"You are aware that Montrose's stepbrother is my son?"

"I...I did not realize it at the time. I do now. You must be appalled at his flagrant behavior."

"Take care with your judgments, Blakely. They may come back to bite you."

"What on earth are you doing?" her father growled.

Amelia recoiled in horror to see her father, followed by the marquis, glaring at her. She had no explanation. She stepped away from the door, lowering her head.

"Go to your room," he whispered roughly. "I shall deal with you later." He opened the door of his study wide. "Radford, if I knew you were coming, I would have made certain I was available," he said, as he stepped into the room.

"No need, I received what I came for, and more than I expected."

Chapter 19

Aunt Libby gasped in astonishment after hearing all that had transpired while she was off visiting with a friend. "The viscount apologized in front of your father and Lady Hastings?"

"Lord Ellington and the duke as well," Amelia said, as she sat across from her aunt in her private sitting room. "When Father called for me, I expected he would be alone and ready to blast me for my inexcusable eavesdropping. Instead, all involved were in the room. Father asked me, calmly, to explain what happened in the library. I do not know if I could have faced the viscount again if the duke had not been there to defend me. Lady Hastings appeared sheepish. She acknowledged she had received a note requesting she join me in the library. She assumed it was from me. When I denied sending it, all eyes went to the viscount. Blakely was visibly uncomfortable. He most likely knew the minute she left her bedroom. He timed his assault perfectly so he would have a witness to an improper liaison."

"Thankfully, the duke's unexpected arrival was as well-timed, and he came to your rescue."

"Indeed, I must have been quite a sight." Amelia sighed. "I have no idea what I would have done if he hadn't arrived at that moment."

Aunt Libby nodded before her lips curved into a

contemplative grin. "I admit I would have loved to see the viscount's face and Lenora's embarrassment."

"It was a spectacle, but I was so relieved to be freed from the fear I might have been forced to marry Blakely."

"From what you tell me, Lord Ellington was on your side as well. No doubt he's grateful that Blakely is not his first son. Ellington's title of marquis will not be wasted on a wastrel. I am aware that Lady Ellington has tried unsuccessfully to find a suitable wealthy wife for him. While the marquis has groomed their older son for the title, his wife has overindulged her second son. It seems even she had grown tired of his excesses and his irresponsible habits. I am not one to spread rumors, but I have heard he has run up debts. I would not be at all surprised if she didn't pressure Ellington to bring their son here, hoping he would gain your favor."

"She will be seriously disappointed. Lord Ellington was outraged at his son's behavior. After demanding he apologize to me, he told him he is withdrawing all his financial support."

Libby's eyes grew wide.

"That's not the worst of it. He threatened to disinherit him if he does not change his dissipating ways and pursue a suitable profession. Blakely appeared to shrink a few inches on his way out. Ellington called for his carriage. They were gone within the hour."

"Can you imagine the atmosphere at the marquis's estate today?" Libby's eyes twinkled with mischief. "To be a fly in a flowerpot or a bee in their bedchamber when Lady Ellington reacts to her husband's edicts."

"Aunt Libby!"

"Have you met the woman? She is a termagant."

Amelia smiled. She would miss her aunt's company when she leaves. "Aunt Libby, I wish you would stay through Christmas."

"This old woman has had enough excitement in the Weatherly household to last me what remains of my lifetime. I am leaving for London in the morning. I have friends I'd like to spend time with before Christmas." She smiled, then grew serious, leaning forward. "I am glad this situation has been dealt with, but you still have much on your mind, my dear. What is it that keeps your smile from meeting your eyes?"

"Do you mean apart from my upcoming meeting with my father for my rude eavesdropping?"

"I don't relish hearing of that scolding, but there is more on your mind."

"I believe the duke is planning to meet with his son."

"Ah, and you are wondering what will come of it."

Amelia nodded. She chose not to divulge that the duke surmised her feelings for his son. "I saw the fire in Lucas Grey's eyes when he mentioned his father."

"Hmm, I trust your keen observance of the young man." Libby lifted a brow. "Good often comes from bad situations and it is not your concern, my dear." She paused. "I must say my visit has been an exceptional one. Although I look forward to returning home, it may seem quite dull after my time spent here."

****

Amelia stood at the door late the next morning, waving to her aunt as the carriage drove off. To her surprise, her father had greeted her this morning and went on with his day. He must want to forget the entire episode.

She spent the next couple of hours wrapping gifts and helping Cook and Jenny make baskets to distribute to tenants. After a light lunch, she sat at her *escritoire* ready to face the unopened mail that had built up while she was busy with their guests. She picked up a handful of invitations. They received many during the holiday season. She expected she may have to send apologies if dates had passed.

Invitations for ladies' luncheons and teas went in one pile and those for her father in another. He had no desire to waste time on opening invitations or holiday greetings. He left it to her to tell him about those deemed important enough for him to follow through.

After opening one addressed to her father, she found an embossed wedding invitation. A spring wedding, perhaps.

The Reverend Benedict Whitcomb requests the honor of your presence at the marriage of his daughter Annabel Whitcomb to Mister Graham Montrose.

She sucked in a breath. "It can't be Montrose? She read the name again. Lucas's stepbrother? Could it be someone with an identical name? It would be too much of a coincidence.

She looked at the date of the correspondence. It must have arrived a week ago. The family name, Whitcomb, was unfamiliar. Why would her father be invited? She rose from the chair and went directly to his study but paused. She was not thinking this through. Was Father even aware that Montrose was Lucas Grey's stepbrother and the man who gambled away her ring? She took a deep breath to calm herself before knocking lightly on the door.

"Come in."

"Father?" She expected to see him at his desk, Instead, his back was to her as he sat in his leather chair by the fireplace.

"I am glad to see you resting, Father," she said, taking the opposite, identical burgundy chair. She noticed he had a drink in his hand, and a brandy decanter on the table nearby, unusual for him in the middle of the afternoon.

"Indeed, it has been. Events have left me much to think about."

Amelia sighed, guilt rising in her throat. She was responsible for much that had occurred. She had been so wrapped in her desperation and confusion she'd given little thought to how everything must have affected her father. And now this invitation could create more tension.

"What is that you have in your hand?" he asked, taking a sip of his brandy before setting it aside.

"We received a wedding invitation. I don't know how to reply. She handed it to him and waited for his reaction.

To her surprise, after reading it, he sat back and smiled. "The vicar is finally marrying off his daughter, is he?"

Amelia quirked her head, stunned that he made no mention of Lucas's brother's name. "Mr. Whitcomb is not our rector. Is this an old friend?" she asked finally.

"He was the vicar of our parish years ago. He married your mother and me as well as my sister and her late husband. We became friends. He was the third son of the Right Honorable Lord of Parliament, Baron Durham. Without a title, Whitcomb went into the clergy after Oxford. He began as a cleric before taking over the vicarage. In time, he moved on to a larger parish. After his father died, he received a generous inheritance. He lives more like a gentleman than a vicar now. We have kept in touch through the years. When your mother passed, he was ill with pneumonia. He sent his regrets. Otherwise, you would have met him." He paused to take a sip of his brandy. "He has only one daughter who must be close to thirty now. He feared she would remain a spinster. He must be relieved she has finally captured a husband. We shall attend. I want to congratulate my old friend. I pray he'll still be alive to congratulate me at the marriage of my daughter someday." He gave her a pointed look but said no more.

Amelia pressed her lips together to avoid a retort. She should tell her father what he had missed in his reading. She smoothed her hands over her skirt before clasping them. "Father, the wedding is next Thursday, two days before Christmas. You had hoped to avoid more revelry."

"Do we have any other engagements from now until then?"

"No. As you asked, I have kept the calendar clear through Christmas."

"Good. I doubt it will be a large affair. It appears to be a wedding of expediency." He curled his lip before setting his drink down again. "Regardless, it is an opportunity to see the vicar. I shall look forward to it. If there is no time to order an appropriate wedding gift, it can be sent after the holidays. On the other hand, a few pounds always please."

"I… shall send back our acceptance." She stood and paused.

"Is there anything else?"

"No. Rest, Father."

She left the room, barely able to breathe.

Chapter 20

"I plan to send our regrets," Georgetta said, setting aside the wedding invitation she received days before. "I need time to forgive my stepson for what he has caused."

Lucas tossed his napkin on the kitchen table and pushed his dish aside. "The situation is over and done."

"Not my anger at what his actions have done to you. You have heard nothing from your work inquiries?"

"No one wants to hire an alleged thief, even to clean out the muck in their barns."

"Oh, Lucas. Graham should be the one punished. If I—"

"You will do nothing, Mother. I have savings that will bring us through the beginning of the new year. I shall figure something out."

"I know your determination. I do not doubt you."

"Molly girl," Lucas said when his retriever barreled in and ran to his side.

Iris entered, red-cheeked, pulling off her coat. "We keep hearing snow is coming, and it feels like it out there." She shivered.

"I would have taken Molly out."

"You needed to spend time with your mother. I have not seen you sit for more than ten minutes without pacing or repairing something. Both the dog and I needed a walk. I will make a good hot soup for our supper."

A heavy rap on the front door drew their attention.

"We are not expecting anyone," Iris said, turning toward the hall.

Lucas rose from his seat. "Warm yourself by the fire, Iris. I'll see who it is,"

As he walked to the door, he pushed away a distant hope that Amelia Pierce would visit again. The image of her wide-eyed surprise that changed to desire when he kissed her remained vivid in his mind. She did not pull away.

He had kissed enough women to know if they wanted to be pursued. He could not pursue Lady Amelia Pierce. She was off-limits. Yet, on his mind constantly.

He would not be seeing her in the spring at the stables or a dinner party in London again. Their paths had no reason to cross. He wanted to banish his need to see her in his thoughts and at the same time, nourish them.

He feared her impetuousness would get her into trouble one day as much as he feared her exuberance would be stifled by polite society's demands.

Jealousy had never been one of his vices but imagining her with anyone else caused sleepless nights. She had bedeviled him when he needed to focus on a lucrative livelihood, not an unattainable woman.

As he opened the door, he combed his fingers through his unkempt hair. Grooming was the furthest thing from his mind these days.

Tom, his old employee from Winston's, stood on the step, shuffling from one foot to the other, his hands in his coat pockets, a wool scarf wrapped snug around his neck, and a worn hat pulled low over his forehead.

"Afternoon, Lucas. You look like hell."

"Good to see you too."

"It's colder than my mother-in-law's heart today," Tom grumbled.

"Indeed, but you are not appearing at my door to talk about the weather. Come in."

"I need to get back. Winston sent me. You're wanted at the stables."

"Why?"

Lucas would not allow himself to hope for his job back, Winston probably needed some clarification on orders he had made or work he hadn't completed when he was taken away.

"I planned to pick up my tools later this week. Are there pressing matters that can't wait?"

"He told me to get you and said no more. The place ain't the same without you."

"If the constable is waiting, he can come himself."

"No, nothin' like that. Winston has business with you. I miss ya, Luc. Bacon-faced Simon is attemptin' to take your place. He don't know his arse from his earlobe when it comes to givin' instruction. Anyway, I'm asked to bring you back with me if you're willin'. I need to warn you, Winston's not lookin' well."

Lucas frowned. John had been struggling with ill health over the past year. He didn't blame him for letting him go, but the work of running the place rested on the older man's shoulders now. He wasn't up to it.

"Go on back. Tell Winston I shall be there directly."

Tom started to turn away but stopped. "I want you

to know I don't believe you've been treated fairly."

Lucas gave an appreciative nod and went inside to change.

Chapter 21

As Lucas rode toward the stables, he couldn't stop wondering why Winston wanted to see him. Did he have business questions only Lucas could answer? He would help in any way he could. Was there a problem only he could solve?

His lips screwed into a scowl as the biting cold pressed against his cheeks. He'd caused John all manner of problems. How arrogant to think he was irreplaceable.

Still, he wondered if Simon or others succeeded in completing all the necessary preparations for winter. Being forced to leave the stables under the constable's guard left him no opportunity to prepare those under his supervision for his departure. Roof repair had not been completed. If Simon was taking over his responsibilities, had he directed the men to finish the patching? Or check for loose boards?

Lucas cursed. Simon was not reliable.

He leaned forward and led his horse into a gallop. The first snow was, perhaps, hours away. The chill in the air was enough proof bad weather was approaching. He had ordered essentials for the winter months, but orders were often delayed or mishandled. Suppliers should be contacted. Winter could be harsh for the horses they sheltered, their provisions, medical needs— He was accustomed to juggle many areas. Simon and the others often required supervision when given a new task.

He gritted his teeth and pushed away the nagging concerns. Winston had been the one who taught him. He knew all that needed to be done, but John's health was failing.

When the entrance to Winston's Stables came into view, he slowed to a trot and rode through the gates. The place was quiet, too quiet. After tying his horse to a post, he climbed the steps to Winston's office. The room was empty. He left and headed towards the main stable, increasing his stride.

His eyes narrowed. "What the..." He rushed forward. "John!"

Winston lay prone on the ground, unconscious. Lucas crouched and pressed an ear to Winston's mouth and sighed with relief that he was breathing. When he lifted his hand that had been cradling his head, he saw the blood. Rocking back on the heels of his boots, he scanned the area. It was past noon. Workers were probably sitting by a fire having lunch.

He couldn't leave him here unattended. He feared moving him might injure him more, but he had no choice. How long had he been lying on the cold ground? Lucas tugged off his coat, removed his shirt, and tied it around Winston's skull. His head lolled back as he raised him up over his shoulder.

To his relief, Tom came around a corner, carrying an armful of wood. He dropped it and rushed over. "Lucas, what happened?"

"I found him on the ground. Ride for the doctor!" Lucas shouted. "I'm bringing him to the house."

Tom gaped wide-eyed before racing away.

Lucas staggered toward Winston's house, set back a distance behind one of the smaller stables and surrounded by trees. John wasn't hefty, but he was dead weight.

Wind whipped at his face as he clambered up the steps to the front porch. He slammed a fist at the door before pushing it open with his boot, causing it to unlatch.

Mrs. Winston rushed toward him and screamed at the sight, her hands reaching out toward her husband's body.

"I found him on the ground. He has a head wound." Lucas said, catching his breath. before seeing his father appear behind her. He gaped, then clenched his jaw. "Martha, where's John's bed? I've sent Tom for the doctor."

A housekeeper scurried into the hall. When she saw the commotion and blood dripping onto the rug, her hands flew to her mouth. "Oh, dear Lord! I'll get water and towels."

"Our bedroom is at the top of the stairs," Mrs. Winston cried.

She reached for Lucas's arm. Radford pulled her back to allow Lucas to move past her.

"You must get hold of yourself, Mrs. Winston," the duke urged. "See that your housekeeper brings bandages. We will take care of your husband. Go now."

Lucas overheard his father's words as he lay Winston down on the bed. Exhaling a long breath, he untied the man's belt and loosened his trousers. Hearing footsteps, he shot a glance at the door. His father entered and without a word, went to work removing the man's boots. Lucas's eyes narrowed,, but he was too busy trying to remove Winston's heavy coat to start an argument.

The duke moved to the other side of the bed, and lifted Winston enough so Lucas could pull the coat down and out of his arms. The housekeeper entered with a pot of hot water. Mrs. Winston carried towels and bandages. Winston's eyes fluttered.

"He is coming to," Radford said, before his gaze drifted to his son's naked chest through the open coat.

Lucas ignored his glare. He drew close to Winston's face. "John, can you hear me?"

He nodded, but his eyes remained closed. Relieved, Lucas stepped back to allow the women to minister to him.

"John has been having fainting spells," Mrs. Winston said, standing by her husband's side as the housekeeper carefully removed the bloody shirt wound around his head. "I begged him to stop working and rest." She rubbed his arm, mumbling prayers as the housekeeper pressed towels on the wound,

"I'll go and watch for the doctor's arrival," Radford said.

With a dismissive nod, Lucas turned his back. He was unwilling to search his feelings about being in the same room with his father after all these years.

Chapter 22

Guilt tore into Amelia's heart. She should have told her father the groom named in the wedding invitation was Lucas's stepbrother. Her conscience might not allow her to keep the news from him much longer. Had she feared he would contact the vicar to warn him of his daughter's intended? Or was it because Lucas was willing to take the blame for his stepbrother's actions?

If they attend the wedding and her father realizes the groom's identity, he might speak up before the nuptials, believing he was saving the woman from a bad marriage. She should have returned the announcement with an acceptance. Her father expected it, but she continued to stall in replying, and the wedding was just a week away.

She continued her daily routine of wrapping gifts and discussing the holiday meals with Cook. With all visitors gone, Christmas Day would be a quiet one, except for her sister and her husband who would return for the holiday meal. None of her busy-ness helped to avoid what she must do. She needed to return the acceptance, and she had to warn Lucas.

With less than three hours before darkness, she called for a gig with the excuse of delivering holiday gifts to tenants while the weather remained stable. If Lucas was not at home, she could at least deliver the sealed note she'd written explaining the dilemma, deliver a couple of baskets to tenants, and be home before dark.

Thankfully, the roads were empty along her route, giving her much time to think. Her life had grown more and more complicated since the day her ring was lost in the hay. No matter how hard she tried to block out the memory of Lucas each time they had met, she could not. Was it love or simply an infatuation? She had never been in love. She'd imagined it would be the consummation of all her dreams for happiness. Instead, she was wound tighter than a ball of yarn most days. At night, in her bed, she tried to unravel all the complications only to wake the next morning with more tangles and snags.

As Amelia drew closer to her destination, anxiety increased. The air grew colder. Had the decision to leave the house been made too quickly? This might be one of those times when she should have at least considered the servant's talk of a storm coming. But if a storm kept them isolated for a few days, she would be unable to do anything.

A loud shout jolted her from her thoughts. Her horse skittered, whinnied, and sidestepped. She pulled at the reins, but the startled animal could not be calmed. She screamed, tugging at the rein until the horse came to a stop, barely missing a ditch.

"What the hell?" Lucas brought his horse to a halt by the side of the gig. "Blast it, man, you do not own the road!" He appeared ready to say more until recognition dawned. "Lady Pierce? Are you hurt?"

Amelia clutched her throat. "No," she said, sucking in a shaky breath before adjusting the fur hat that hung half off her head.

He dismounted, and tossed the reins over a nearby branch before jumping up on the gig. He nudged her aside with his hip before Amelia could breathe another word. After taking the reins from her hand, he drew the horse and carriage back onto the dirt road.

"Do you realize you turned that bend without looking?" He swore as he stopped the gig at a safer area on the road. "What are you doing out at this time of day in a gig with the temperature dropping? Are you batty?"

"I beg your pardon. Where were you going in such a rush? I am not entirely at fault." Amelia snapped.

The dread that had gripped her was replaced by fear of the man crowded beside her in the small seat. He wore a stone-hard expression, his eyes appeared black as slate, his brows nearly covered by wet, tousled waves.

"Women! Always trying to find a way to get out of their stupidity."

She crossed her arms tight against her and glared.

He huffed. A corner of his lips slowly curled up. "I admit I was not paying attention either. I apologize for my rudeness. Where are you going this late in the day?"

"To see you."

"I am the last person you should be coming to see. I am nothing but trouble for you." His gaze wandered from her eyes to her lips. "You need to go home. The weather is changing for the worse."

His concern for her safety did not excuse the bitter tone of his words. She had not seen this side of him before. She should be frightened, but there was something more in his expression. He may have been heading toward home but at such a hard gallop, it was as if he were running toward or away from danger.

Amelia tilted her head, confused. "What is wrong? You were riding as if you were being chased or challenged."

He slumped his shoulders and took a hard breath. "I came from the stables. I found John Winston lying on the ground, unconscious. He's in serious condition. The doctor is with him now. Perhaps I should not have left, but I could not stay, not with him there."

"The doctor?" His last utterance sent a chill through her.

"And the Duke of Radford," he said through clenched teeth.

"Your father. I don't understand."

"He was in Winston's house when I brought John in. I have no idea what he was doing there. Perhaps he was trying to fix things like he did at the jail. I do not need his help."

"Your father cares about you," Amelia said in a cautious voice.

Lucas glared at her. "You know nothing."

Amelia shrunk back at Lucas's rage, but she could not stop. "Have you ever spent time with him?" She could not forget the pain she heard in the duke's words when she listened through the door of her father's study. Nor could she forget how he had helped her.

Lucas sneered. "I never laid eyes on my father until I was five or six years old. At that age, I didn't understand my place in society. My mother's protective nature kept me from loose tongues. I had a vague memory of going to London with her to my grandfather's funeral. My grandmother had traveled to the country a couple of times to see us, but my grandfather refused to come. Still, Mother wanted to pay her last respects to the man who had disowned her. Shortly after we returned home, my father came to the house."

Lucas gave a dismal shake of his head, looking down the road as if he were reliving the past. "My mother never said a bad word about him, but she never spoke of him either. When I was old enough to ask why I did not have a father, she avoided the question. As is the nature of a child, I repeated the question. She said finally, 'Your father takes care of your needs, but he has a different life he must live." She refused to say more and changed the subject if I asked." He pushed his hair back and looked away. "I don't know why I am telling you this. You need to get home."

She ignored his dismissal. "His visit must have been not only difficult but puzzling to a young child. Seeing him today must have stirred up these memories."

Lucas gave a sardonic laugh. "When he visited, my mother brought me to stand before him. He knelt, stared at me, and ruffled his fingers through my hair. I clung to my mother's skirts. I remember that. A few years later, when I was maybe nine or ten, my mother's sister came to visit with my two older cousins, both a couple of years older. We were sent off to play. They were the ones who told me what I was called in the world. They had heard their parents talking about my ignoble birth. They enjoyed repeating what they had heard before they pushed me down in the dirt, kicked me, and laughed, before begging me not to tell."

Tears sprang to Amelia's eyes. "How cruel children can be. And you did not tell on them?"

"No, their punishment would not have taken away

their words. I saw my father a couple of other times from a distance as I grew older. Once on a trip to London, I saw him leaving his carriage to go into the gentleman's club. Another time, he was a spectator at the stables. He may not have known I was working there. The one thing I knew and still do. I loathe him."

"Because you believe he deserted you and your mother?"

Luke dragged his fingers through his hair and smirked. "We were better off without him."

Amelia was not certain his answer came from his heart.

"I'm worried about Winston. He's been more of a father figure for me."

Amelia fingered a stray black lock of hair that fell over one of his eyes.

He grasped her hand. "Beware. You are tempting danger, Lady Pierce."

"Please, call me Amelia."

He gave her a crooked grin. "I should not have told you all that. You caught me at a disadvantage."

"I am glad you did."

He drew her hand to his heart before letting it go and leaning back. "You say you were coming to see me. Why?"

Amelia sensed his deliberate detachment as he handed her the reins he had been holding in his other hand. She had been so absorbed in his story she had forgotten for a moment the reason for her trip. "We received an invitation to your stepbrother's wedding. I was unaware that my father knew the bride's family. He told me to send our acceptance. He did not recognize the groom's name. I fear if he does, he might interfere, believing he is protecting the bride."

"And you wanted to warn me."

Amelia lowered her head, uncertain even now if her reasons for coming made sense at all. "Your actions demonstrated you care for your stepbrother. Was he not the one who should have been punished or jailed?"

He lifted her chin and drew his lips close to hers before cursing under his breath and dropping his hand. He jumped to the ground. "You need to get home and stay away from me."

She leaned toward him in her seat. "There is more I need I tell you."

"I don't want to hear anymore. Has anyone ever told you that you are impulsive and rash in your decision-making, and also a pest?"

"More often than I could count," she murmured. "I have also been accused of speaking out of turn. Lucas, your father did not know your mother was in a family way. Did you know that? He loved her."

He fisted the sidebar of the gig. "How would you know that? You are a foolish romantic, prying into matters that are not your concern."

Amelia shuddered at his icy words but the thoughts that had been circling her mind for days needed to be brought into the light. She rushed on. "You must accept that men with titles have tremendous responsibilities. Much is demanded of them. They are responsible for so many. My brother has been groomed for the nobility. He will inherit my father's title and the expectations that go with it. Honor, obligations, and suitability in marriage is not a pleasurable thought to him, it is a demand. Privilege also carries heavy burdens."

"And you will marry someone suitable as well."

Amelia turned away as tears threatened.

"Say no more. Be honest with your father. We do not plan to be at the wedding. If I see Graham, I shall tell him to beware. Best be on your way." He started to walk away but turned back. "How do you know my father well enough to speak in his defense?"

She could not tell him she had listened in on his plea to her father or that he was responsible for saving her reputation. "I have nothing more to say."

A drop of snow landed on her nose. She looked up as tiny droplets fell. "Oh, no, I will be in so much trouble."

"Damn." Lucas looked at the sky as flurries fell.

"I must leave." She fisted the reins to turn the horse.

Lucas grabbed her hands. "Now it is too dangerous. This snow will only grow worse and the wind is picking up. Come to the cottage and wait it out."

"No one knows where I am. I am supposed to be delivering Christmas gifts." Desperation caught her breath. She brushed away the snow that had already collected on her sleeves. "I need to get home."

"Do you want to end up in a ditch?" Lucas thundered as a burst of wind caused the gig to sway. Ignoring her protests, he grabbed his horse's reins and tethered them to the back of the gig before jumping back onto the seat. "My mother and her housekeeper can serve as chaperones until we can figure out how to explain your whereabouts." He pulled the reins from her hand and led the horse onto the road.

Amelia dropped her head in her hands. There was no escaping her father's wrath this time.

Chapter 23

Neither spoke as the snow fell harder and the wind grew fierce. Lucas focused on the road ahead while his thoughts remained on the stubborn woman beside him. Left to her own devices, she could create more havoc than a pack of squirrels let loose in a lady's bedchamber. Despite her reckless behavior, she left the confines of a warm home to warn him.

She needed to stay away from him, yet he wanted to be her protector. Why? Her presence in his life had brought one nightmare after another.

His attraction turned to anger as he dwelled on her words. How dare she tell him of his father's noble responsibilities. Worse, Radford loved his mother. Where would she acquire such information? What was she not telling him?

Graham's wedding will quite possibly be spoiled once her father realizes the groom's identity. He shot a glance at Amelia. Her face was half-hidden beneath the snow-covered collar of her coat. His mood turned from anger to bewilderment. She had gambled her respectability to see him. Days ago, she had arrived at the cottage on horseback to find out the truth of her lost ring, and now to warn him of possible consequences at Graham's wedding. Passion smoldered each time they were together. Unless he was delusional, she felt it too. She had gotten under his skin and into his heart.

Feelings had no place in the reality of who they were. The daughter of an aristocrat cannot be matched with the illegitimate son of a royal, a mistake of birth. Her future husband must be acceptable to polite society and her family. He could imagine her father's fears that his estates would fall into the hands of a miscreant. They could never be together. Yet, he could not blot out his desire for her, to protect her, and never let her go. It was madness.

He thought of her lips, moist and waiting for his kiss. She had not turned away. Was her rebellious nature urging her to taste the forbidden, the opposite of what her upbringing demanded? No, he had had enough encounters with the wives of the nobility who lured his attentions as a distraction from their ancient or boring husbands. It was different with Amelia. Her eyes when they met his, did not hold simple flirtation or deception. He thought his heart was hardened to love, but she had captured it.

Impossibilities swirled in his mind like the wind gusting the snow in their faces. His gaze darted again to Amelia. She stared at the road ahead with quickened breath and shoulder slumped. Suddenly irony struck. What if it was true that his father had loved his mother, rather than simply using her as Lucas had believed? Had both he and his father fallen for unsuitable matches?

His father was groomed for the dukedom and all it demanded. His mother, the daughter of a poor tradesman was unsuited in all ways. He, a bastard in love with an earl's daughter. In love? He had never thought those words before, certainly never uttered them. Never felt the feelings that stirred in him when he thought of Amelia.

"Damn!"

"What?"

"Nothing."

Amelia covered the lower part of her face in her collar again, allowing Lucas to return to his revelation. The scorn he had for his father that had hardened his heart was wearing away. No the truth remained. Knowing they could never marry, Radford took advantage of his mother, and left her pregnant. Lucas cared enough for Amelia not to ruin her for a more suitable match.

But how would he explain her presence in his house tonight?'

Chapter 24

Amelia trembled but not from cold when Lucas led her into his cottage. She was living a nightmare of her own doing and the outcome promised a worse storm than the one outside the door.

Iris met them in the hall. Molly squealed in welcome until Lucas commanded obedience. With a whimper. the dog returned to her bed.

"You must be chilled to the bone, my dear," Iris said, having overcome her initial astonishment at seeing Lady Pierce. "Lucas, your mother is napping. Shall I wake her?"

"Let her be until I return. I need to take care of the horses."

"I shall have Lady Pierce settled by the fire before I prepare a room for her."

"Please, do not go to such trouble," Amelia pleaded after Lucas left the house. "As soon as the snow stops, I must be on my way."

"This storm is not leaving any time soon," Iris said, helping her off with her coat. "I am sure you could use a few minutes of privacy, and you need to get out of that wet skirt. The hem is frozen. You are close to Georgetta's size. I shall find something dry for you to wear, not of such high quality as you are accustomed, but warm and serviceable until your skirt dries."

"I apologize for adding to your work."

"It is no trouble at all. Take a seat by the fire. I shall bring some hot tea before I prepare the room."

"Thank you, Iris."

The housekeeper was kind enough not to ask about her unexpected appearance. Would Lucas's mother be as accommodating? She imagined her father's rage when he discovers her whereabouts. He would not beat her. That was not his way. He would send her away, perhaps disown her.

"Hot tea will help take the chill out of your bones," Iris said, returning a few minutes later. She placed a tray with tea and small cakes before her. "I shall be back to collect you."

Offering a grateful smile, Amelia waited for the housekeeper to leave. She poured a cup of tea, grasping the cup with two hands when her fingers trembled too much to lift the dainty cup with one. The hot liquid was welcomed. After a few sips, she stared blankly into the fire. As the minutes ticked away, she realized she was helpless to do anything.

She rose and walked to the window. Icy snowflakes flew against the glass. The sky had turned a darker gray and the land was immersed in white. How would she go home or even get a message to her father? With the suddenness of the storm's fury, he may have already sent men out to find her.

She pressed her fist against her lips, trying to suppress the terror building inside her at the cost of her disobedience. What would her father do when he realized Lucas brought her here? She had to think of a logical reason for traveling this far and finding shelter in his home. She was well-chaperoned, but how could she explain traveling beyond her father's holdings? She was not merely drowning in a river of impossibilities but caught in the snarled roots and broken limbs of her foolish actions.

She paced as she tossed out one poor explanation after another.

"Milady, the room is ready for you."

So caught up in her fear, she jumped at the sound of Iris's voice.

"I didn't mean to startle you. Come, my dear."

Iris led her to the back of the cottage and a small, cozy room. A candle was lit on the bedside table and a skirt was spread out on the bed's quilted coverlet.

"Let's get you out of that wet skirt. I'll hang it to dry by the kitchen hearth."

Too embarrassed by the entire situation, she didn't argue. Once she was dressed in a simple gray wool skirt, Iris left. Amelia looked about the bedroom. Apart from the bed and night table, the room was simply furnished with a bureau, a small desk, and a chair. Lace curtains hung in the two small corner windows. A rug, woven of varied earth colors, covered the pinewood floor.

She paused at a small oval mirror that hung above the chest. She looked as bad as she felt. Wet straggled strands of hair had loosened from the chignon her maid had carefully styled that morning. She pinned them back as best as she could. Rosy cheeks, raw from the cold, did little to hide the anxiety written on her countenance. She turned away and picked up the knitted wrap the maid had left and draped it about her shoulders.

Taking a shallow breath, she swallowed hard to press down dread and gather calm before leaving the room. A sudden ruckus echoed through the hall. She clutched her throat. Was it her father? No, more likely, Roderick. He must have been out searching for her. The memory of him dragging her off Lucas in the stables only a few weeks before shot through her mind. Hurrying from the room, she nearly collided with Lucas's mother.

Georgetta stared wide-eyed at Amelia, but there was no time for explanations. Amelia followed her as she rushed to the front hall.

Snow flurries blew in from the half-opened door as Lucas stood face-to-face with the duke, his voice raised above the howling of the wind. "I insist you leave now."

"For God's sake, shut the door!" Georgetta shouted above Lucas's raised voice.

Lucas's gaze darted to his mother. "He is not welcomed here."

Georgetta swept past Iris, the housekeeper's mouth agape, and passed the two men to the open door, shoving it shut before standing between them. She appeared diminutive against their tall figures. "I have no idea what is going on but it is time to talk, not shout."

"He has no right to be here!"

"I ask that you grant me a few minutes of your time," Radford said calmly.

"And we will allow it," Georgetta said.

Amelia was awed by the sight and confused. Her family had not discovered her whereabouts, but the fury on Lucas's face washed away any sense of relief. More surprising was Georgetta's visage when she looked up at the duke. Was she imagining the tenderness in her expression?"

"My driver is waiting. I shall not take long."

"You must tell him to come in out of the cold," Georgetta said. "He can go into the kitchen with Iris and get warmed up."

Lucas appeared outraged as he glared narrow-eyed from his mother to his father. He fisted a hand against the wall, his lips pressed together as if he were damning up a flood of rage. When the duke left, Georgetta put a hand on her son's arm. He shrunk back from her touch.

She crossed her arms and raised a stubborn chin. "Lord Radford's appearance, drenched from the blizzard at this hour, and Lady Pierce's presence, wearing one of my skirts, needs to be explained. We will go into the parlor and have a civil conversation, so we are all enlightened on this unusual scene. Iris, when the duke returns, take his outerwear and offer his driver a hot drink."

Lucas took Amelia's arm and led her into the parlor. "I apologize you had to be a witness to this spectacle."

"I am as much a reason for this spectacle as His Grace. Your mother is right. We need to talk."

Lucas guided her to a chair. He refused to sit. He strode to the fireplace and stood stiffly with arms crossed. When the duke returned, he chose the opposite side of the hearth near where Lucas's mother had taken a seat.

The look Lucas gave him would make another man flinch. Radford appeared unmoved by his son's obvious resentment.

"Your Grace, you must have an important reason to travel here in a storm," Georgetta said, gazing up at him from her seat.

"As Lucas already knows, I was at Winston's Stables." He turned to him. "You will be relieved to hear that John Winston was awake and resting comfortably when I left."

Lucas's hardened expression did not waver. "Why were you there in the first place? Interfering in my life once again?"

"Lucas." His mother frowned. "Allow him to answer your question."

"I admit I was interfering. A few days ago, after I learned you had been dismissed from your position unfairly, I had a meeting with Winston. Today, we were finalizing some business when a worker called him away. Thankfully, you arrived and found Winston. He is very grateful to you, as is Mrs. Winston."

"I will see him for myself tomorrow. What business did you have with him aside from your interference?"

The duke grimaced but did not avert his eyes from his son. "After we discussed the unfortunate situation of Lady Pierce's ring," he said, glancing at Amelia, "he told me what had occurred with customers. He had no choice but to let you go or lose valuable revenue. He sent one of his men to find you today, as you know. He wanted to apologize after hearing the truth of what happened. He realizes he is too old to run the business. In his words, 'you are the only man he would trust to run it, even better than he.'"

"We would have worked things out, without your intervention."

"Perhaps, but a problem remained. As much as Winston wanted to take you in as a partner, his waning health over the past year forced him to reconsider. He could not retire unless he sold the entire establishment. He knew you did not have the funds to buy the business. He has high respect for you and did not know how to tell you. With the reactions from his wealthy customers at your arrest, he had no choice but to concede to their demands so he could sell the business at a profit. I offered to buy him out. We signed papers to that effect before he was called away. I will have no part in it, nor will my name be involved. You are the new owner. It will be up to you whether it succeeds or fails. I trust you will make a success of it."

Lucas glared in disbelief. He turned from the hearth, rubbing his forehead. "It is your business, not mine. I would have continued to work hard and build the business so that Winston could retire without worry."

"I believe you would have done just that, son. Unfortunately, Winston's health problems would not allow him another season of work. I want no part of the business. It is yours."

Chapter 25

Lucas wanted to hate him. He had called him son. He never expected to hear those words from his father. With his heart pounding in his chest, he wanted to spit out all the hateful things he had saved up to say to him one day. But he had never expected to hear his father praise him or believe in his abilities.

He had imagined all kinds of scenarios when confronting him, but this did not fit. He eyed Amelia, remembering what she had told him about ducal responsibilities and more that he hadn't wanted to hear. He crossed his arms about his chest, glaring at his father with narrowed eyes.

"I should be grateful for your generosity. I should be grateful you have taken care of my education and our financial needs; despite how much we must have been an embarrassment to you and your family. My mother and I have been a financial cost to you. You did not need to offer anything else. If Winston Stables is mine to manage, I will enlarge the establishment and make the business even more successful. I shall pay you back for your initial investment and more until I owe you nothing." He ground out his last words, unable to contain or extinguish the anger built up over the years.

"Enough!" Georgetta edged close to his father's side.

To Lucas's shock, his father drew an arm around

her waist."

"What the hell?" Lucas stepped toward Radford.

"Lucas, stop. It is time you listened to me," his mother said. "I told you I went to see your father while you were imprisoned. During those awful days, he and I had much to talk about and to find what we had lost so many years ago."

"Georgetta, allow me," Radford said, his voice tender. "I love your mother. I have always loved her, no one else. Circumstances made it impossible for us to be together."

"You left her without regard to her condition," Lucas snapped. "How could you allow her to be shamed by her family and hidden away?"

****

"Lucas, he did not know!" Amelia blurted, unable to remain quiet. She had been holding in the tension growing inside of her, but the pain on Lucas's face was more than she could bear. Seeing the stunned reaction to her outburst, she bit into her lip, wishing she could take back her words.

"How would you know that?" Georgetta asked, her tone curious, not threatening.

Amelia closed her eyes. Would she ever learn to quell her tongue? She stood and looked at Georgetta and the duke before releasing a breath she had been holding in. "I must ask His Grace for forgiveness. When you visited my father and was led to his study, I followed. Your son's imprisonment had so much to do with my actions, and I knew so little about what was happening to him, I…" She swallowed. It felt as if her heart was in her throat. "The door to father's study was left partially opened."

"And you did not leave?" the duke said, his brow furrowed.

"I should have." She lowered her eyes for only a moment, swallowing down the guilt that rose, before shaking it off. She could not allow her shameful behavior to stop her from what needed to be said. "I heard your raised voices within. I stayed. I am ashamed to say. When you found me running from the house, I was able to trust you and accept your help because I had eavesdropped and listened to your admissions to my father. I heard it all. I understand we do not always have a choice as to who we fall in love with. You were willing to give up the dukedom and all it embraces for the woman you loved as well as fight for your son's freedom. I…"

Embarrassed by her outburst, she turned her gaze toward the nearby window, wishing she could dissolve like the snowflakes that were hitting the glass. She shouldn't be here, involving herself in their family issues. Her father was right. She acts without thinking. Would she ever learn?

To her surprise, Georgetta smiled, and wrapped her arms around her before gazing at her son. "She heard correctly, Lucas. I did not tell your father I was in a family way. I knew he would come to me and walk away from his responsibilities. He did not know you existed until years later. By then, he was married to another. He did what he could so we could have our own home. I could never remove the stigma placed on your birth and for that I am sorry. All your father and I could do to make amends for the burden you would have to carry as our child, was to nurture you with the best of what each of us could give, without breaking the vows we made to others. You have made us both proud, Lucas."

She gazed up at Radford with love in her eyes, fingering the pendant necklace she wore, his gift of love so many years before. "Your father and I never stopped loving one another. We both desire not to waste any more years being apart. I did not know how to tell you, especially after you lost your position." She returned to Radford's side. "No doubt you need time to consider all you have heard. Unfortunately, another matter is at hand." She glanced at Amelia. "Have you any idea what Lady Pierce's presence here will cost this young woman? I assume she was not kidnapped or brought here against her will."

"I am wholly at fault for my situation," Amelia said. "I fear my father may have already sent men out to search for me."

As she spoke, a loud rapping on the front door drew their attention.

"Oh, no!" Her hands flew to her mouth.

Lucas caught Amelia's eye as if he too, expected to see her father's men at the door. "I will see to the visitor."

Muffled voices in the hall gave no hint of the intruder. Amelia pressed a hand to her chest to calm her pounding heart and dropped into her seat.

A few minutes passed before Lucas returned, but no one from the Weatherly estate appeared. Instead, Graham Montrose, storm-worn, and wearing a sheepish expression, entered the room. Lucas followed. "My stepbrother, Graham," Lucas said, with a grimace. Instead, he returned to his place by the hearth.

Graham, wet and red-faced from the cold, cleared

his throat. "Forgive my intrusion. I thought I might beat the storm when I left London. Instead, it won the contest. It is in my nature not to think things through as I ought."

Despite knowing Graham's part in Lucas's imprisonment, she couldn't help but feel some sympathy for Montrose, especially since she could relate to rash behavior. She saw the confusion written on his face at the odd gathering. The crackling of the fire, the sound of the wind, and the silent tension emanating from each person created an eerie atmosphere. The duke's downturned lips held contempt while Georgetta's anxious expression darted from her stepson to Radford and back. The duke, hands fisted to his sides, took a step toward Graham. Georgetta reached for his arm, giving him a look that begged restraint. Amelia held her breath.

Georgetta broke the silence. "Why are you here, Graham?" Her lips pinched in disapproval.

Graham took a couple of steps further into the room, bowing slightly at the sight of the duke. "Your Grace, Mum, Lady Pierce, Lucas, I did not expect to have such an audience. In truth," he gazed at Lucas, "I came to ask if you would do the honor of being my best man at my wedding."

There seemed to be a collective, relieved sigh in the room. His simple request seemed absurd, his dumbstruck expression nearly laughable with all that had gone on before his arrival.

"I believe you have more to say and to confess," Georgetta said pointedly.

Graham, with a bowed head and in somber words confessed all. "I have no excuse for my lack of self-control. I make careless and costly gambling bets when I have indulged too much. My callous actions caused Lucas undue harm and brought pain to my stepmother who has always treated me with kindness. All I have to offer is my deepest apologies. I have confessed, as well, to my intended, as Lucas demanded I do. Thankfully, she has a forgiving nature, having been brought up in the church. Forgiveness I do not deserve after my disloyalty to Lucas and Mum." He gazed at both. "I also apologize to you, Lady Pierce, who I treated with disdain simply because you were born into a wealthier class. My intended pointed out to me that I judged your position in society with the same disregard we of lesser means are judged."

His apologies did not remove the scowl on the duke's face. Georgetta's features softened.

"I have been aware since your youth, Graham, of your mischievous and impulsive behavior and as you grew older, your assorted schemes. Most of the time, your wayward tendencies have caused me to roll my eyes and send up a prayer you would reform. This time, what may have seemed to you at the time to be petty thievery, caused much grief. Forgiveness is difficult." She gave him a steely glare. "I do believe you are repentant. I have not forgotten the times you protected Lucas and your willingness to take your father's blows meant for him. I am not excusing your pilfering, but you have my forgiveness."

"I know it is undeserved. You have always been kind-hearted to me." He turned to Lucas. "You insisted I confess my actions to my intended. I expected Annabel to run to her father and call off the wedding. It was a humbling experience. She spent a great deal of time, to the point of exhaustion, I admit, telling me the benefits of cleansing my soul. I have no doubt she will keep me on the straight and narrow."

Lucas's lips curled up, but he gave no reply. Graham quirked his brows. His gaze darted to the other occupants in the room and back to Lucas. "I have interrupted an unusual gathering. Indeed, none of my business. I should leave, but the roads have become impassable."

"Sit, Graham," Georgetta said. "You will stay the night. Lucas, we must decide how we can help Lady Pierce."

"First, I need some answers." Lucas glared at Amelia. "What did you mean earlier when you said my father helped you? Why did you run from your house and why was he involved? Is this another incident where he has interfered?" Lucas eyed his father with animosity.

Amelia frowned. She would not feed his need to stay angry at the duke. "The visiting viscount, the same one who won your ring from your stepbrother through stealth, attempted to compromise me. Your father saved me from being forced into an unwanted marriage."

Lucas's eyes widened. "What?"

"Yes," she answered boldly.

Listening to Lucas's mother and Montrose's fiancé's reaction to his confession, gave her inner strength. These women were not afraid to speak up to stubborn, insensitive men. Her nerves had been teetering on the edge of a cliff of worry as each minute passed. After what she had observed, she could no longer stifle her objections to Lucas's stubbornness, despite the new arrival. She sprang from her seat, squared her shoulders, and faced Lucas. Stopping a few feet away, she stood with her elbows jutting out and her hands fisted firmly to her waist.

"Lucas, I am grateful for your father's intervention in freeing you from jail. I am deeply sorry it was my father whose accusations placed you there. Thankfully, you are free, but you remain imprisoned with hate and unforgiveness. Your father and mother are deeply in love. And do not call me a 'romantic' as you did previously. I can see it in their faces. They both love you and have loved you in the best way they could, considering their different circumstances." Her voice softened. "I know too well aristocratic demands placed on sons and daughters that we are unable to defy. Privilege, as your stepbrother said, may offer wealth and power, but brings restraints that can be unbearable. When I saw no way out of the vile viscount's attempt to compromise my reputation, your father came to my rescue."

"What is this viscount's name?" Lucas snarled. "Did he harm you?" His hands fisted. "I want his name."

"He has been dealt with," the duke replied.

"No harm came to me. Lucas, I care…"

She stopped, realizing she nearly poured out her feelings for him. She gazed around the room. Everyone was staring at her. She returned to her chair.

"Forgive me for interrupting," Iris said. "I have a nice, hearty soup on the stove and warm bread just out of the oven."

Lucas gaped at Iris. Laughter burst from him. Others joined in.

Amelia's mouth dropped and soon she was

laughing too. Perhaps, she had made a fool of herself, but she felt free suddenly from the emotions that had built up in her. Her father would need to understand. Somehow, everything would work out. Would it not? Or did she lose all sense of reality?

Iris stood in the doorway waiting and smiling at the group.

Georgetta caught her eye. "Iris, thank you. Your timing is perfect. We shall be in shortly."

After the housekeeper excused herself, the duke frowned. "Lucas, you are the son of my heart, my only son. I regret the law will not allow you to inherit my title, but you will share in all that I have. Lady Pierce speaks the truth. You have always been loved, and you are the product of love. Your mother and I have spent too many years apart when we belonged together. I have asked her to marry me." He took Georgetta's hand. "She would not give me an answer for your sake. I am asking for your blessing. I promise I will love and care for her for all the days I have left."

Lucas rubbed a hand over his face before looking at his mother and his father. His chin softened. His shoulders relaxed. "I want nothing but happiness for my mother. I see the love when she looks at you. You both have my blessing."

Amelia's eyes filled with tears at the healing between father and son. Lucas's parents were wrapped in each other's arms, their faces glowing with happiness Graham Montrose smiled at the couple. He had been truly repentant. Lucas would now be a man of business and accepted as a gentleman of property and worth. In her heart, he always had worth.

"Please, excuse my interruption," Graham said.

"Lucas, if I might ask again, would you be my best man?"

The room broke into needed laughter once again.

Amelia joined in briefly until her thoughts returned to her dire situation. What grief was she causing her family at this very moment? Perhaps, her father might consider that she had found refuge with one of his tenants. Or, worse, he might fear she was in a snowdrift, lost, even freezing to death.

"Now, the matter of Lady Pierce must be dealt with," the duke said.

"I would much prefer if all of you would call me Amelia. I feel the honesty shared in this room and the understanding deserves informality between us."

"I have become quite fond of you, my dear, and I appreciate your words to my son on his behavior." Georgetta gave Amelia a broad smile.

"I agree with her, Amelia," the duke said. "I admire your spunk. Now, considering your situation. My driver, Zachary, is young and robust. If I can borrow a horse from my son, I shall send him to deliver a note to Lord Weatherly, letting him know you are well and safe. When the storm subsides and the roads are passable, you shall return home in my carriage. Your father will expect an explanation sooner than later. I shall provide one. We must also deal with the relationship between you and my son. Your reputation is at stake. A double wedding might be in order."

Amelia's mouth dropped.

"Are you not in love with my son? He is most definitely in love with you. I see it when you look at each other. If I am wrong, please tell this old fool."

Amelia looked at Lucas and he returned her gaze.

Neither spoke.

"That settles it. The two of you will not go through what Georgetta and I have had to live with all these years. Polite society can go to hell. Love takes precedence. We will work this out. Societal rules, including children born out of wedlock, have been broken since before King Henry II." He smiled at Georgetta. "I would enjoy some of that hot soup your housekeeper has been stirring up. I suggest that we, and Mr. Montrose, retreat to the kitchen and leave these two to talk." He reached for Georgetta's hand. "I shall compose that note to Lord Weatherly and send my man on his way."

Georgetta took the duke's hand before addressing her stepson. "Come, Graham, we are not done with you yet."

Left to themselves in the parlor, Amelia avoided Lucas's gaze and walked to the window. "I no longer hear the wind howling, and the snowfall appears lighter," she said, looking out at the snow-covered landscape, nervously clasping, and unclasping her hands at her waist. "A note from the duke should give my father some peace of mind. No doubt I have caused him much worry. Is it not wonderful that you and your father appear to have come to a place where you can talk? I hope you are pleased he and your mother have pledged their love once again. They both appear happy. Indeed, good has come from unfortunate circumstances." She raised a hand and brushed away loose strands of hair from her cheek, tucking them behind her ear. "I was so sorry to hear about John Winston's ill health and then to have both your father and your stepbrother appear at the door when you have barely rested from being so unfairly imprisoned. I pray you will forgive my father. And me as well. After all, if I had not been so careless as to lose my ring. And, oh my. My mind can barely take in all that has occurred. And now it is getting dark. I do think we must get that note written sooner than later."

As she rattled on with hardly a breath, Lucas drew closer. His nearness and his silence were not helping her at all. She bit into her bottom lip and closed her eyes.

His hands brushed her upper arms, gently at first and then bolder as he urged her to turn around to face him. He released his right hand and placed it on his heart.

"I have much to express, in here," he said softly, "and little to say with certainty about all that has happened. I need time to sort it all out. My father, my mother, my life, more. One thing I can say with certainty is that you are a headstrong, willful, impulsive, young woman, and a badly behaved daughter. I can only imagine the turmoil you have created in your family with your actions. If by some miracle your father will accept me as his son-in-law, I hope I can give him a measure of relief by taking you off his hands. If you will have me." He touched a finger to her dampened lips as she was about to speak. "I am in love with you, Lady Amelia Pierce, my Amelia. I believe I have been since you fell into my arms in the hay. I cannot regret the ring's journey if it leads to our union."

Tears rolled down Amelia's cheek. She sucked in a breath, gazing into his eyes. "I love you too," she whispered.

"Is that a yes?"

"Yes. Oh, yes!" She squealed when he lifted her off her feet and twirled her around in his arms before kissing her very, very well.

Epilogue

Aunt Libby sipped her brandy while gazing about the comfortable parlor at the Radford estate.

"I see a gleam in your eyes and a touch of a smile. You appear content and pensive," Amelia said.

"I am savoring our delightful dinner and pleased to be in such good company." She smiled at the duke and duchess. "And, admittedly, I was reflecting on the startling events over these many weeks."

"You are not alone, Libby," Amelia's father said, as he relaxed in a chair by the fire. "The weather outside reminds me of another snowy night and a missing daughter."

Amelia winced as Lucas's parents cuddled on a nearby sofa before gazing on her husband who stood by the hearth. Amelia would never want to relive the moment she arrived home in the duke's coach after the snowstorm. With a few omissions, His Grace had explained how he had discovered Amelia trapped by the snowstorm. They found refuge at the home of his intended and thought it best they wait out the storm—a partial truth.

"Amelia, I still ponder the telling of your mysterious disappearance from delivering Christmas packages to spending the night in the Grey's cottage. Naturally, I was relieved you were safe." He gazed at the duke, who gave a reluctant smile.

Resting her head on her husband's shoulder, Georgetta arched a brow.

"Father, I was quite safe, well chaperoned, and all turned out well."

"I should say it has," Aunt Libby said. "Two lovely weddings in short order."

"And quite unexpected," her brother said. "When Lucas asked for my consent to marry my daughter with his father standing by, I was dumbstruck. I could never have imagined Lucas Grey on his knees in my study proposing marriage to my daughter. His proud father stood by grinning as if it were a normal circumstance rather than a shocking spectacle."

Amelia stifled a chuckle. She remembered her father's mortification. After she accepted Lucas's proposal, her father asked to be left alone. Eventually, he accepted there was little he could do or say when she declared her love for Lucas.

"If you recall, Charles, I made it clear my son was now the heir to my fortune and the owner of Winston Stables."

"Yes, yes," the earl harumphed. "I could hardly reject his suit. Waiting for Banns to be posted was hardship enough for the two of them. Amelia refused to wait until spring for a formal wedding."

"Come now," Libby cut in, "the double ceremony of Lucas and Amelia, William and Georgetta was breathtaking. We witnessed such happiness, not unlike your marriage to your wife, and all officiated by the same reverend."

Georgetta laughed. "We kept Mr. Whitcomb quite busy, having just married his daughter to my stepson, Graham."

"Graham appears to be a changed man," Lucas said, rolling his eyes. "At least for the time being. She appears to have the patience of a saint."

"All turned out well," Amelia repeated, as her husband strode from his place by the hearth and sat beside her.

"I spoke with John Winston after the ceremony," Libby said. "He was recuperating from his fall but refused to miss the wedding. He has such admiration for you, Lucas, and expressed regret for his actions during the ring debacle."

"He had little choice," Lucas said, fingering a strand of his wife's hair as she smiled up at him. "When Father negotiated with Winston to buy the business, I detested his interference. Both Amelia and my mother corrected my distorted view and distrust of my sire." His lips curved into a broad grin as he and his father exchanged meaningful nods. "John was thrilled that I was the new owner. He is now relishing retirement."

"You must be busy preparing for the spring opening, Lucas. That is, if this harsh winter every comes to an end," the earl grumbled.

"Quite busy, especially with Amelia's plans." Lucas drew her closer.

"My daughter's plan?

"An equestrian training facility for ladies and eventually competitions," Amelia said, her heart welling with pride.

"I could not refuse my wife's request for women's events. She is too headstrong to take no for an answer."

Her father relaxed back in his seat and giving a symbolic wipe of his palms. She was Lucas's problem now. Yes, Aunt Libby was right. Marriage brought freedom and so much more.

"It is time we retired, my dear."

Amelia blushed, recognizing the glint in her husband's eyes. Lucas reached for his wife's hand as they both rose and wished the others a good evening. Tomorrow, they planned to return to the country cottage that was Lucas's home, their home now. The duke had urged them to settle into one of his estates, but they refused. Amelia loved the quaint cottage and the time alone with Lucas.

Even before they entered their bedchamber, Lucas had already loosened the ties on the back of her gown. After closing the door behind them, he swept her into his arms. In his embrace, she had all the happiness she could have ever dreamed of.

And more.

Thank you for purchasing
this publication of The Wild Rose Press, Inc.

For questions or more information
contact us at
info@thewildrosepress.com.

The Wild Rose Press, Inc.
www.thewildrosepress.com